FIT FOR CONSUMPTION

FIT FOR CONSUMPTION

STORIES
BOTH
QUEER
AND
HORRIFYING

STEVE BERMAN

LETHE
PRESS

For

Jeff Mann

who has never denied his cravings for food and men.

———————

When the waiter leaned over their table immediately after seating them and gravely announced: 'Tonight is special, sair,' Costain was shocked to find his heart pounding with expectation. On the table before him he saw Laffler's hands trembling violently. But it isn't natural, he thought suddenly. Two full grown men, presumably intelligent and in the full possession of their senses, as jumpy as a pair of cats waiting to have their meat flung at them!

— "Specialty of the House" by Stanley Ellin

Mr. Beard leaves no survivors.

— "James Beard, Authority on Food, Dies"
The New York Times

STORIES

IN SUMMER BROKEN

G HOST STORIES HAPPEN AT ODD hours, not just October midnights; on a humid June evening, four princes returning from abroad, freshmen come home for the summer, drive the winding and sparsely-lit back roads, between dark fields and sullen farmhouses, the scent of the day's manure fading until it's a whiff rather than a stink as they ride with all the windows down because the Beetle's air conditioning is long-dead, the service-engine light burns bright, and the only sound is their gaiety, no music blares and the speedometer's needle falters; the boys are freshly intoxicated and they know police like to lurk in the dark and summer is newborn, it's the solstice, and who wants to spend the longest night of the year in county lockup? When summertime is newborn so many princes come back to their dominions wary of who might have usurped their roles at court; Mullim and Charles, Nick and Frenches, all tipsy to tanked from the cheap beer served at the Northampton party they abandoned too too early because Frenches ran into his ex-boyfriend in the arms of this year's prom king: Frenches's stocky frame, fifteen pounds fuller than last year, expanded, like a threatened pufferfish in a home aquarium, and all eyes at the party watched as he circled his ex- and gestured with a beer bottle warmed by a white knuckle-grip and threats of where he wanted to shove the bottle. His best friend Mullim stepped into Frenches's line of sight and calmly told him not to care about someone's sloppy seconds, and Charles, not-quite-a-best friend, embraced both of them and announced loud enough for all at the party to hear that the ex- wasn't just seconds, he was as sloppy as the gravy boat passed around on Thanksgiving, and then Nick, who alone wasn't a local but hailed from an even more distant land, namely New Jersey, and was Frenches's current beau—he actually refers to Frenches as Prescott because that's how he goes at college—Nick blocked both ex- and king from taking two steps closer. Nick made sure he cocked his head so all would notice the thick scar that ridged along his unshaven jawline, and to those who didn't know it was the result of life-saving surgery he had when he was fourteen, it promised a Prince Who Can Handle Trouble. The king of the prom stuck out his hand and thumbed down, spilling froth and suds from his plastic cup (mostly suds: whoever manned the tap was a rank amateur) onto the dirt. The princes were banished, but they departed with rude pomp and style, cussing, throwing their bottles and cups, flipping middle fingers to all the boys and girls as they drove off, heavy on the horn. Only several blocks later did Mullim, behind the wheel of the Beetle, which was once his older brother's until he was given something new and shiny, realize that he'd forgotten to turn on the headlights, and they laughed at how stupid drunk they were and decided it would be best to travel the quieter but longer pockmarked asphalt rather than risk the smoother, more patrolled highway. As they pass through gloomy Whatley, though, on this shortest night of the year the sky is a breathtaking pallet of light blue rising to indigo, Nick demands one of them explain why they all call Prescott Frenches when he can't even properly spell *croissant*. Mullim: What happened back in elementary school was Prescott, who went by Scotty then, became the Prince Everyone Dared, and in the cafeteria, every day for a week straight, saw a different lunchtime dare culminating with eighteen little packets of yellow mustard added to his hot dog; what he held aloft as his prize was more mustard than wiener or roll, and he ate every bite, his fingers gunky, t-shirt stained, chin slimy. Charles claims he came up with the nickname. And Frenches, who's always happy to be the center of attention, wiggles his tongue and makes a joke about how big is Nick's wiener and, despite their intention to be quiet, there are howls and laughs. Charles hushes them in that insincere manner drunk people have, saying they're loud enough to

wake the dead, and Mullim knows he's referencing last night, when Charles
came over and they watched a scary movie, supposedly an excuse to lie close
together in bed, and would the spark ignited years earlier, did it still smolder?
After so many months apart, did the heart grow fonder? Nick asks if the
back road they're on is haunted; back in New Jersey, Nick lost his virginity
one night in high school while looking for ghosts along the most infamous
stretch of road in the entire state, and he looks out the open window at the
many trees that are becoming but silhouettes against the sky, that one ahead
and on the right looking like something from an old horror flick, maw open
to swallow the Beetle, boys and all. Mullim's the Hand-Me-Down Prince
and even his ghost story he can't call his own but was told by his brother: if
you look in the rearview mirror you might catch a glimpse of a car way
back, driving down from the horizon, and some nights the car gets closer
and closer, and by then, well, it might be too late, as you realize it's an old
car, something sleek from the seventies, as green as a tropical serpent, you
can hear the roar of its engine, which leaves the smell of hot metal in the air,
and if the car begins to follow you, if you realize it's following you, then its
headlights wink out—and Frenches laughs as he shouts out, That's what we
did, driving back from the party—and Mullim says You don't dare take
your gaze from the rearview mirror for long or the demon car's high beams
flare, burning like coals, its engine roars and you're blinded by the glare,
forced off the road. The road's lines, painted on the macadam, the guardrails,
even the telephone wires strung from pole to pole along the periphery, all
glimmer when a rare passing car's lights reveal them. Like gossamer and
cobwebs are wont to do. And then you're dead, says Nick. But Charles lifts
off Mullim's Red Sox cap and slips it over his own head, turning the brim
around. The ghost's not a demon car, Charles says. A neighbor who moved
away, a friend of hers or maybe a cousin, she saw the ghost on this road. She
was driving all by herself, and she was nervous 'cause she had been
drinking—just like us, Frenches calls out; Nick stifles the next few words by
shushing him with a palm over his lips and Frenches works his mouth to
suck on a finger or two—when the girl left the bar where she'd been tossing
back beers, she accidentally backed her car into a dirty and rusted pickup,
and there'd been any number of Massholes in the bar that night who could
own that junker. But she doesn't stop, she doesn't scribble down even an

apology and slip it under a wiper blade, no, she stomps on the gas and heads out of the lot. It's a night she wishes she had stayed home instead of gone out, and she swears she'll be good and she'll be sober for the rest of her days if she can just make it home that night—and Mullim leans over and says in a low voice to Charles: Would you rather we stayed home? Charles offers a sad smile, not even a half-smile, the same expression he gave Mullim the night before, after Mullim looked up from beneath the bedsheet, face and scalp all sweaty, lips messy, and Charles was still panting but scrolling through his phone. The girl, Charles says, is halfway home when she sees the headlights in her rearview mirror and, while she tells herself there are plenty of people who're driving home that night, like her, she knows in her guts that it's the guy in the pickup truck wanting payback, so she starts driving a little faster and every time she passes a little sleepy side road, she starts mumbling, Please turn, please turn, but the lights behind don't and they're getting closer and closer, so she speeds up to stay ahead of the guy and soon she's driving over seventy through Whatley... Nick: And then? Charles: Oh, suddenly there are blue flashing lights swirling behind her. Yep, all that time, the car behind her was actually a sheriff. Nick laughs at this because, on the night he had gone looking for ghosts but found none and ended up sweaty and stripped bare in the backseat of a Dodge, a cop knocked on the fogged window and almost scared him to death; the other boy was, for all intents and purposes, scared straight and wouldn't even drive Nick all the way back home but stopped at the end of his block and denied everything the next day, week, the rest of the school year, including denying Nick's existence; Nick guessed it was a way to earn back your virginity, and he sort of did the same thing when Prescott told him that, though he had dated a few boys, he'd yet to do *everything*, because the last guy insisted he'd only top and Prescott's high-school besties had told him once how awful their first time bottoming went, Charlie, when he gave up his ass, had texted all of them that pain scale they ask little kids to use, pointing to the emoji expression that goes with how much it hurts, with a squiggly arrow aimed at the penultimate grimace, so Prescott was as anxious as a feral cat, so Nick told him that he was a virgin too, and hey, it went kinda nice, much better in a little dorm room bed than the backseat of a car. Charlies tells how the girl pulls over to the side of the road and begins to cry, thankful tears that it's not the pickup truck guy coming to rape and kill her,

STEVE BERMAN

embarrassed tears because she feels like a total idiot for getting so worked up
and speeding, and bitter tears because the last thing she did need right then
was a ticket for a couple hundred dollars and maybe the cop will understand
if he sees a sobbing girl behind the wheel. The cop, meanwhile, is taking his
time getting out of his car, and she thinks this is just to torment her, but the
thing is, she doesn't know what had happened to the cop days earlier, when
he was doing his cop-thing hiding by the side of the road, aiming that speed
gun, hoping to make his quota, when he sees this car from out of state and
it's passing the slower cars, narrowly missing several by just inches … this
is a two-lane road, you see that sign, like that one, *Don't Pass* … so he does
his duty, though he thinks that they're gonna try and outrace him, so he's
shocked when they pull over, nice and easy. Only, they're a couple of meth
heads and tweaked out of their minds, and when he leans in to ask for their
license and registration he gets the barrels of a shotgun in his face, and they
let loose with both barrels, and cars passing by, they actually see the cop,
poor guy, fly backwards in a spray of gore. Charles chuckles as he's the
Naughty but Nice Prince, likes horror movies and body counts, had more
detentions than the other three princes combined, but he doesn't want to be
all bad or even mostly bad, has deep and painful moments of guilt whenever
he hurts someone he leaves but, like the girl in the car, knows that the next
night there'd be another drink, another *oops* and accident, and more tears.
He came by Mullim's last night to watch a scary movie, and also because he
missed Mullim; they came close to dating once or twice, but Charles knew
that fucking Mullim would be, at best, second best because Prince Hand-
Me-Down is nowhere near as hot as his older brother, Tam, who would
tease Charles whenever he came over, by lifting up the bottom of the tight
t-shirt to wipe at a handsome face, sweaty or not, knowing that Charles was
captivated by the sight of one-two-three-four, damn, five-six abs. Charles:
The cop comes up to the driver's side and the girl rolls down her window,
and it's late, she hears the cop mumble something, of course he can't really
talk right because he doesn't have much of a mouth anymore. And Nick is
shouting Damn, and Frenches grabs him and squeezes him tight. Frenches
is overcome with not fear but love, he loves these guys so much, it can't be
because of all the beer, he must have a heart that matches the stomach that
digested eighteen little packets of sour mustard without dying. Charles
chuckles: And she notices something odd about his uniform—Charles

5

shouts in Mullim's ear that the cop's shirt is soaked in blood. Mullim shoves him away, but since they are all sitting in a Beetle, it's not like there's much room for Charlie to go. Frenches sees the expression on Mullim's face and realizes that, while he loves them all so much, there's not so much love amongst them all, he read Mullim's texts to him this morning, couldn't really answer then why Charlie had run off suddenly, but oh, now he has suspicions, so he throws a beefy arm around Charles's neck, and he thinks, *Mullim deserves better*, and *Charles is the one who always wants better*; none of them dares say it aloud, but they know Charles wants to get fucked by Mullim's big brother, who boasted when Mullim came out to his family one night that he always knew Mullim was gay because all of his friends were faggots, and the naengmyeon on the table became cold and the Tam was grounded for two weeks, and in those two weeks he made all their lives miserable, and Mullim didn't want either Charles or Frenches to come over his house, not with the way Tam would taunt them—Tam reeked of varsity football and wrestling and could have beaten the shit out of any of them, making them anxious little kids cussing and flipping the bird, much like they all did back at the party tonight. The party tonight ... Frenches realizes that Nick would have stood up to Mullim's brother, called him a cocktease, made him look away, back down. Frenches is convinced that something happened between Charles and Tam the other day. All because of what he saw on Charles's phone at the party. So Frenches knows what ghost story he must tell: The real ghost, it's this kid who you'll see walking all by himself along the shoulder of the road. He's dead but doesn't realize it, he's not even watching where he walks, so he strays into the middle of the road, like a deer, which is probably how he died. He's busy staring at his phone—and as he's telling this, Frenches is sliding a hand into the pocket of his shorts, getting out *his* phone, which he hands off to Nick, who winks at him, because he can guess what needs to happen—and most people just drive on by without realizing the boy is dead either, but the scary thing is, sometimes a person in the car gets a message from the boy and whatever you do, never, ever text him back because that's when he'll show up ... in the car with you! Charles jumps as his phone begins to ring. Even Mullim is surprised and swerves a little. They all laugh, even Charles: You assholes, such assholes. Frenches has already grabbed Charles's phone, and despite the way Charles is calling out

No, no no no, and trying to reach over the seat for it, now that the phone is unlocked, Frenches can easily hunt and find the photos he caught Charles gawking at when he thought no one was looking earlier tonight. And there's the pic and there's more than one, and they're terrible, a shot of a hand grabbing the crotch of gym shorts with the message *miss this dontcha?!* and sweet Nick who gawks at the pictures asks, Who's this guy? and a fast swipe through the lower half of an Asian face makes Nick ask Mullim if the pics are him. Mullim now pays more attention to Charles's phone, held aloft in Nick's hand, rather than the road and the car begins careening. There's a sudden blare that rends the air as a truck—how could they not have seen it barreling down the road?—warns them, and Charles has to grab the wheel to keep them on the road. What is that doing on your phone? Nothing, nothing, Shit, oh shit, Who is that guy? Nothing happened. Nothing happened! It's is the worst thing Charles could say; it's the worst thing anyone could say on a lonesome country road at night because it's an admission, and that's an invocation for something terrible to happen, a guarantee. Nick screams, There's something on the road. A dog as big as a deer but shaggy and dark-furred, with a terrier's filthy beard, and the lights from the car reflect in its eyes, making them glow orange, hanging orange eyes. Mullim brakes and the car lurches in the middle of the road. He's crying and while Charles is asking What, why, how the fuck is that a dog?. Mullim is asking about the pictures on Charles's phone, but he won't answer, keeps talking about the dog, even leans out the open window and yells at it to move. Mullim yells at Charles to get out of the car. What? Get out of the car ... I can't believe you ... you fucked Tam ... (Frenches thinks, *Tam probably fucked Charles, fucked him silly*) ... there's a fucking dog the size of a pony out here ... good, good, why don't you fuck that too? (*Bet the dog is hung like Tam*, thinks Frenches.) Charles makes a show of unlatching his seat belt as he glares at Mullim, as he opens the door. I didn't mean for any ... for anything to happen, I never wanted ... aww, fuck this, and Charles is out of the car and standing there at the edge of the road. Frenches reaches over and puts a hand on Mullim's shoulder: You can't leave him like this, he's a touch fucked-up, but you can't strand him here. Where's the dog? Nick asks, and he's looking back and forth, peering out all the windows. Charles's face is streaked with tears, but he starts walking, not in the right direction but back the way they came. Nick anxiously asks, Where's the dog? Frenches says, Get in the car, man! Mullim starts the car and turns it around and he starts pacing Charles who's staring straight ahead. Mullim's asking him to get back in the car and after the third attempt, he actually pulls ahead onto the shoulder, and Charles, who has never been nimble and is less so while tipsy, stumbles into the car's bumper and scrapes his knee. Mullim gets out of the car. Guys, do either of you see the dog?, Nick says, and his awkward tumble out the door onto the grit-strewn asphalt has an audible crunch and he cradles his wrist. Mullim stabs Charles with his own phone and then Charles punches Mullim, knuckles colliding with nose. Mullim yells out and nearly crumples but then Charles is there, holding him up and saying how sorry he is, sorry for everything, sorry just so sorry. Mullim feels warmth and wetness on his lips and chin, and believes his nose must be broken. Charles strips off his shirt and offers it to Mullim to staunch the bleeding. Both boys get back into the car, Mullim is clutching a sweaty, blood-stained, beer-stained shirt with one hand, can't put the car into gear and so Charles works the gearshift and everyone hears the transmission groan, Mullim's steering is off because he can't see, but Charles says he's way too drunk to even get behind the wheel, and everyone feels smothered by the tension, and wounds old and fresh. Nick winces, cradling his arm to his chest, as Frenches demands they go to a hospital. They pass a farmhouse with boards across the windows, brush growing out of the porch. Around the next bend their headlights reveal a state-trooper car idle and quiet beside a farmer's fruit stand. Stop, Mullim, stop, let the trooper take us to the hospital, Nick asks. None of us should be driving, none of us would make it home now, and so Mullim flashes his lights at the trooper and then parks the car on the gravel-strewn shoulder, and the sedan rolls towards them. Everyone's face is streaked, and when the trooper leans an arm on the driver's door Mullim sees

bloodstains on the trooper's sleeve and hand
and he isn't sure if the blood has dripped
off his nose
or
was
it always
there.

THE BALM OF SPERRGEBIET IS THE KROKODIL

"Some of the evil of my tale may have been inherent in our circumstances. For years we lived anyhow with one another in the naked desert, under the indifferent heaven."
—*T.E. LAWRENCE*

WE HAD SURVIVED SO LONG in the abandoned buildings of Kolmanskop because this was a forlorn desert, made so with constant gales carrying fog and grit. A paradox of nature sheltered five of us while the world beyond the Namib went mad.

Sand covered all things. The sand of the Namib retained the bite of gravel while never abandoning its mercurial nature. It forced open every door—every structure in stately Kolmanskop welcomed the desert. This had once been a mining town of German settlers where the wind revealed and hid the shells of humanity. I have walked through a ballroom without chandeliers, a doomed ice factory, and the remains of a hospital. I discovered the tracks I made the prior day gone, erased by the wind, which scratched plaster and color from walls erected more than a hundred years ago when diamonds had been discovered.

I read once that nowhere else on this Earth is wind this constant. It stole words from mouths and ears. It threatened to blind. We had to cover

9

any water, any meals, or else the sand covered them like an inedible spice. I always had the taste of the desert in my mouth, a sensation not so much unpleasant—one became inured to any flavor, however first repellant, after a thousand swallows—but the texture was an irritant; the grit wore down my teeth, my palate, so that anything I chewed became bland. The desert weathered my face, my hands, and any exposed skin. Wrists and necklines were chafed till bloody, became scarred over, then debrided, in a perpetual cycle of scarring. We all stank, changed clothing only when needed, and became familiar with the odors of the others when downwind. I have not had a shower in nearly two years and my body's topography is no longer the same. Hygiene mattered only if it jeopardized our meager food and drink stores.

When the Internet died—and I still cannot comprehend how anything so rampant, so rife, could die ... any more than imagining every bird across the globe becoming mute forever—and smart phones became lobotomized paper weights that would no longer even indicate time or date, I had thought some terrible war had happened. Blinding and deafening Africa south of the Sahara had been collateral damage.

Torschlusspanik made me decide that my life as a logistics clerk for African Development Bank in Windhoek was over.

I looted books from the public library. I walked in and took what I wanted. No one stopped me. Soldiers watched me with disinterest from the nearby Alte Feste, a monument to the colonial era pressed into service as a shelter.

South: I went on roads that would lead me home. As an Afrikaner, a prodigal son of Bloemfontein and a coward. But the car quickly ran out of gas and I had to set out on foot. Trudging along worn asphalt roads, I could not avoid the other refugees. Some travelled in the same direction, some left South Africa. I heard that the City of Roses had fallen to some biological weapon that left buildings full of gall rot and moulds. My parents were Calvinists and sure in their predestination; so I didn't mourn them. I turned back instead.

I entered the Namib Desert because of two German men and their dog. As a young man I read and reread Henno Martin's *Wenn es Krieg gibt, gehen wir in die Wüste.* My male peers preferred football, the females an undistinguished *plaasroman.* I knew that one could survive the desert, what could be eaten, and how to find refuge. I began my journey through

Sperrgebiet National Park, the Forbidden Territory, believing it would be uninhabited. My fears of contamination left me, taken by the strong winds.

Others, though, had similar ideas. We arrived from different directions and lives. We met at Kolmanskop and stood and stared. Impasse or concession? Cook is Ovambo, a lapsed Lutheran, and brought a goat-drawn kitchen of pots, utensils, even bags of millet. His younger brother, Toivo, wore a corporal's uniform, shouldered a rifle, and squinted often. A White Namibian, Ludwigsone, claimed to be a journalist of late who had been covering prejudice at local hospitals. He had stolen first aid supplies including a great deal of codeine.

We made a pact. We suspected others would come: tribesman, urban refugees. We admitted that any of us may not last long, that isolation might become an unmanageable burden. We looked long at the cleaver, the rifle, and the needles in Ludwigsone's bag. I shared the story of an older brother who had been an addict. I saw no need to tell them the truth. Enough years had passed that my perception and distinction of brother and lover had no depth.

And so Cook brewed krokodil. We stored it under the sand, above the floorboards of several buildings.

That was, by my estimate, fifteen months ago. I found purpose through everyday chores. With purpose came contentment. At night, I read. I hoped to memorize all of *Seven Pillars of Wisdom* and *Selbstbehauptung des Rechtsstaates* before I died. Both books were dear to me as apologetics for the role of strife in the world.

The fog flowed inland from the coast and brought us water, condensed on plastic tarps stretched taught like sails. Our diet, the occasional lizard but mostly insects, beetles and the termites that we found beneath the beautiful and short-lived fairy rings made in the coarse sand, left us with loose teeth and clothes. A treat was goat milk and porridge. We did not hunt game for fear of wasting bullets or wandering too far from Kolmanskop.

At dawn Ludwigsone spotted four figures stumbling through the fog. The wind on occasion revealed the old rail line that led to Kolmanskop; they must have followed the cracked ties and burnished steel.

As we readied ourselves, I watched Cook use a handkerchief to cover fresh abscesses on his little brother's upper arm. Toivo would be abandoning us soon, though we may need to amputate first.

We called out to the trespassers—that was what we named any who came upon us—in Oshiwambo, in Afrikaans, in good German, and in poor English. I waved to bring them closer. They carried nothing. I guessed them Bantu or the like. Their clothes were ragged; they had traveled farther than any of us. Two swayed from hefty stomachs—one man fat, one woman clearly pregnant—and were led, hand-in-hand by a pair so lean that the foursome's stagger up and down the dunes bordered on the comical.

The wind brought back their cries. A scattering of English amid other words that none of us understood.

Salt covered their lips. Why they had not licked the crystals loose, I could not guess. Perhaps that would draw fresh blood.

Experience had taught us to keep our gestures and words welcoming. We guided them towards two particular buildings: I lightly pressed a hand on the woman's back and motioned to the left, while the others suggested that the men stay to the right. The gaunt man leading the woman did not want her to part ways. Cook and Toivo smiled and broke the man's grip on her hand and gestured again for the trespassers to separate. We offered them water. They saw Cook's cleave and Toivo's rifle. They had no choice.

I swept grit off the building's only furnishings, a single chair and table. I told her to rest and I would bring water.

I took a moment to look in at the others, to make sure that nothing amiss had happened. I had worried that the heavy-set trespasser might be difficult to handle, but now I saw how ill he was, bloated and hampered by his round stomach rather than possessing a bullish girth. The makeshift tray I brought had a jug of water, a chipped mug, and a capped syringe. The last I moved to my back pocket. We had seven thin syringes but lacked the bleach to clean them. None of us were really clean, inside or out.

"You traveled far," I said to her as I set the tray down.

She nodded. Her eyes watched me pour. Once you have been in the desert, you can never look away from running water. It became a living thing that seduced your every sense. The sight of it, the sound, you would hallucinate the taste, the smell, the sensation of it flowing down your throat.

"Why did you come to the Forgotten Territory?" I held the mug.

She mumbled. No food for days can lobotomize a person. I finally understood she was saying, "We are missionaries."

12

She wore no cross. Nearly all of Namibia was Christian, and the desert beetle had no ear for Jesus's teachings.

I asked, "Is your heart full, drawn out in prayer unto Him continually for your welfare?" I had heard the Mormons say such nonsense.

She nodded. "I am full. Dof'mru has filled me." Her hands parted her tattered clothes to show the bare, distended skin of her abdomen. More bloody lines of salt whorled around her navel.

Was Dof'mru one of her companions? Perhaps it was some Bantu name.

"Do you know Ahtu?" I had to ask her twice before she shook her head. I handed her the mug.

We, the gestalt, had agreed to no women at Kolmanskop. We worried they would bring jealousy and discord between us. I had as much use for a woman as my icon Lawrence. I had guessed that the others were suspicions of my tastes and were thankful that I always volunteered to suffer the female trespassers.

I walked behind her as she drank. Thirst had caused the veins in her bared neck to rise to the surface. I did not hesitate—I had never before hesitated whenever I was needed to plunge the hypodermic.

She cried out but the krokodil worked fast. Faster and more potent than morphine. Her limbs twitched, giving the illusion of a struggle, but it was really easy to lower her body to the sand.

As I went to work—stuffing a dirty rag into her mouth, which caused her caked lips to bleed; shutting her jaw and pinching her nose shut—I distracted myself with reciting a favorite passage from *Der Vater eines Mörders:* *"Mit seinen braunen, festen Händen hatte er auch zog einmal die Brücke auf Franz 'Instrument um einen Bruchteil eines Millimeters, so dass für eine Weile die Geige war schöner als zuvor klang."* German was an unrivalled language. I wished I could have seen the Rhineland but I doubted what I would find now would be anything like I wanted it to be.

The very first time I had to dispatch a refugee, I fumbled around until I broke her neck. Nearly pulled a muscle in my back. Suffocation was simpler, though more time-consuming.

I felt a spasm travel through her body. Unexpected, unwarranted. I looked to her face. Her eyes were still, glazed. I am sure they remained unseeing. But her belly and chest roiled. Despite my grip on her mouth, her jaws were being forced open. A tip of a tongue pushed aside the rag.

A tongue colored not pink but a shade of red so deep as to first appear black until it met the air. It slipped farther and farther past her slack jaws. My own mouth must have hung open in shock. It was no tongue.

Sand slid through my fingers, flew up as my boots kicked, and I retreated a few feet to watch the segmented body escaped the dead woman. Her bloated stomach collapsed. The thing, larger than my entire arm, resembled a caterpillar in shape, except no tiny legs in the fore, no eyes of any kind, just a lamprey mouth to indicate the head, but the rear did have the false feet of butterfly larvae. Above a gaping anus, two branches ending in something akin to pipe organs wheezed.

That awful sound broke the stupor brought on by shock. I struck the thing first with the water jug, then smashed the mug and stabbed at it with the largest shard. Its blood burned my skin; the pain was not from heat but the bite of salt poured on an open wound.

I didn't stop until I had nearly torn it in half. Both my hands and forearms would need to be bandaged. Lost to anger, I kicked the dead trespasser, the thing's host, before running off to warn the others.

The other three trespassers had been drugged and chained to a wall for interrogation. Ludwigsone slapped the gaunt one and asked about Ahtu, an unfamiliar name several who had wandered across Kolmanskop uttered like a mantra—we had once thought it might be a warlord or a new disease like Ebola, but were still unsure.

I told them about the woman and the parasite. We began to pass words of concern between us while staring at the fat man's belly.

"They said they came to preach from Natron which is a lake, I think, in Tanzania," Ludwigsone said. "It is so alkaline people believe it petrifies animals, but it just coats the dead with salt. And the water is blood-red from small organisms that live in the lake—"

I grimaced. "This was not small!"

He shrugged. "I don't know what you saw. I don't like the sound of it, but the lake's a fuckin' flamingo preserve."

Cook ripped the shirt from the fat man, whose head rolled, his mouth so dry that it hung open without any spittle dripping down to the sand. We could see the skin of his stomach filthy with raw and ruddy patches of salt.

"That ain't good," said Cook. "Ain't right, and I ain't having it here."

Toivo shrugged. "Then we kill."

We were all in agreement. Then the others saw what slithered out of the fat man. Cook swore. Ludwigsone wiped his glasses clean. Toivo took a syringe of the krokodil and walked away.

We would never consume the bodies of trespassers. We were afraid of contamination. But we did drag the corpses to a site and let winds carry the scent to scavengers, like we did with our feces. When you are hungry, what does it matter if you eat a jackal or a dung beetle washed clean?

But none of the scavengers went near the bodies. The must have known it was tainted meat.

Ludwigsone began bothering the rest of us with questions, new ones, about what might have happened to Africa, to the world. He muttered "Ahtu" to himself like a trespasser might. I have also heard him speak of Dof'mru but do not remember telling him anything that the woman spoke.

The trespassers tainted Kolmanskop.

Cook told me that Ludwigsone had asked if they could travel north together, to the edge of the desert, that answers were needed. He did not ask me because I am White also; he needed someone dark-skinned to accompany him so he could convince folk he was born in Namibia and not a foreigner. Cook had refused. He would not abandon his brother, not while he still breathed.

Of course, Ludwigsone might quicken Toivo's parting with more krokodil. *Torschlusspanik* made men do awful things. Cook was smart and warned Toivo not to tell Ludwigsone where he was sleeping off the drug. But he did tell me.

We held the funeral the following morning. Cook recited what little of the Bible he knew. Ludwigsone remained quiet. I read Lawrence's dedication from his opus, but I could not bring myself to say aloud the line "And the blind / Worms grew fat upon / Your substance" because the memory of the parasite haunted each of us.

I expected the next evening would find me all alone in Kolmanskop. The others wouldn't return from their quest with answers. I do not want to know what they might find. Rather, I would busy myself with the chores life demanded: harvesting the water, gathering the food, and reading until the pages fall from the books. I might tire and take the needle myself before more trespassers find me. I am Afrikaans and have become cruel, but I am like no monster I have ever seen.

CAPTURING JOVE LUNGE

OH, HOW THE CAB STANK. A rattling heater raised from the scarred seats the ghosts of dog-cheap cigars the driver must have smoked over decades. Like the one he was savoring now. Trapped in the back, Gus rolled down the window to let fresh air, cold and late-January sharp, seep inside.

He regretted the boss insisting he take the train from Manhattan to Providence rather than drive the Rover. Saul had sworn that the best way into this case was for Gus to appear down on his luck. Which meant a visit to a rag shop to buy some fellah's former Sunday best. Underneath his trusty peacoat, though, Gus's immense frame strained the suit's threadbare patches.

The cabbie took a turn too sharp. Brakes squealed as the car struggled with the snow-covered road. The seams tore in Gus's sleeves as he stretched his arms to keep from tumbling about the backseat.

When the house came into view, Gus whistled his appreciation. Saul had been square with him about the artist's taste: something out of a storybook, with lots of shingles, a crooked roof, and plenty of eaves. Gus expected Boris Karloff to be sitting on the front porch with his hands cupped around a steaming mug of joe.

The cab slowed on the cobblestone driveway, which circled a frozen fountain. The driver chewed around the stogie stub and muttered that he'd return the next night for Gus, who grabbed his bag and had barely stepped out of the car when the cab drove off, one rear door swinging like a tarnished goldfinch's broken wing. Gus considered pitching a rock at the cabbie's back window, but he made it a point not to earn trouble while always anticipating some.

He would have to demand that Saul send him someplace warm and inviting for the next job.

A pair of custom-made knockers, brass fists gripping lightning bolts, decorated the gaunt doors. Their metal felt colder than a moll's heart and rang out like gunshots when Gus struck them against the wood.

A few minutes later the door cracked open. One rheumy eye glared at Gus, who cleared his throat. "Yeah, Mr. Moiren is expecting me."

The door opened wider, revealing more of the dark-suited butler, a thin man in his late fifties with a blood-red eyepatch hiding the worst of the damage suffered by the right side of his face. The man's rigid stance suggested he had once served in the military. A Great War veteran, Gus suspected as the man moved aside for him to enter.

The butler accepted Gus's peacoat. "Master Moiren will receive you in the greenhouse."

"That ain't like the poorhouse, is it?" Gus made sure to bray like an ass; "Nothing's a worse tell than a man's laugh," Saul always said, and if Moiren and the help thought Gus was a moron, it would make finding the girl easier.

"You may leave your bag here," the butler said as he hung the coat on a nearby rack. Gus counted the other coats. None looked like they belonged to a spoiled rich girl, but that didn't mean Samantha Kingsford wasn't still here.

A grandfather clock, hidden by the many shadows of the foyer, chimed three in the afternoon. Mournful sounds.

The house's drafty interior wasn't much warmer than the outside. Most rooms weren't lit. Frost caked the windows. Gus rubbed his palms together. "All right, pally, lead the way." His breath rose in the air.

"This way" said the butler, as he lifted one hand.

Rich men didn't impress Gus. He knew they hid behind their money. Or used it as license to be vicious and petty. But Saul liked dealing with the wealthy, especially men like Donald Kingsford, father to one wayward daughter who needed returning.

"Big enough joint for just Moiren and you." Gus paused to stick his head up the flue of a blackened stone fireplace roomy enough to roast a pig like they did in Polynesia. But the hearth was cold. What good was such trappings if they weren't used?

"The master entertains on occasion."

"This be one of those occasions?"

The butler said nothing. He didn't need to. Gus had already caught a whiff of perfume, expensive perfume, in the house's draft. And this house lacked any feminine touch, so he doubted there was a Mrs. Moiren. No, Samantha Kingsford was here.

WHEN HE WALKED INTO THE massive space confined by a lattice of fogged glass and damp copper, Gus shook off the house's chill like a soaked dog. The humid air reeked, a bit like an outhouse in July, a bit like Brussels sprouts steaming on a plate. Gus had been born in the city; Central Park was the only spot on Earth with so much green. The closest he'd ever come to the jungle was admiring Johnny Weissmuller in that *Tarzan* talkie. But Moiren's greenhouse had taken a chunk of South America or maybe Africa and held it prisoner in Providence. Gus didn't spook much, but he knew he didn't belong surrounded by all the wild foliage.

A voice from on high called out, "Welcome." Gus looked up. Half-hidden behind shoots and wide leaves, a scaffolding covered part of the greenhouse wall. A man, wearing a bruise-colored satin smoking jacket and a ridiculous hat that looked like it should be made of glass and covering a stack of donuts, not red felt with a tassel, stepped towards the railing. He held aloft a struggling rabbit for a moment, then dropped the animal down into the brush. "Our Jove Lunge, the Man of Daring, has arrived." Nestor Moiren—Gus recognized him from the photos Saul had spread over his messy desk—clapped languidly with limp wrists.

"The name's Gus."

"As if it matters." Moiren began descending a flight of stairs. His slippers echoed through the greenhouse. "How are you finding Providence?"

"Cold."

"Yes. It is." Moiren had a puffy face but thin lips. Gus had seen other men wear that same smirk, usually right before they threw lead around or tried to shiv you in the guts. "Did your man tell you what I require?"

Gus rubbed his square jaw. Saul had a number of guys working for him. Gus normally was called when the job required brawn and intimidation, not retrieving runaways. But Saul thought that a guy playing off Moiren's fascination with big men would have an easier time getting the girl back. "Said you needed some hired muscle."

"Indeed I do, but not the sort you're used to providing." Moiren turned to the butler. "I think the *Howl of Black Shuck* will do nicely."

The butler bent with an audible creak and left the greenhouse.

"That name I called you ... Jove Lunge—"

Gus shrugged as he slipped off his jacket, which cost him a whole dollar. Sweat had begun to seep down his back and armpits.

"—have you never read the Jove Lunge adventure stories?"

"Never made it past the racecards." Gus loosened his collar. "So, who you want me to slug?" When people thought he was just some sap, they'd grow lazy ... and show their hand sooner. Gus could tip a car but he was no easy mark.

Moiren's chuckle sounded like a dying man's last wheeze. "A rare *Nepenthes*, but that comes later." The man stared at him. "Here we are." Moiren lifted a hand as the butler returned carrying a framed painting.

Gus paid little mind to art—he did appreciate the photos in *Iron Man Magazine*. But the hoity-toity museums all over Manhattan were too quiet for his liking. Not that there was anything quiet about *Howl of the Black Shuck*. The hackles rose on the back of Gus's thick neck as he glanced at it.

One glance at the figure of Jove Lunge, his uniform flayed to shreds by the panther in his path, told Gus that Moiren liked his men strapping, bulging muscle and taut sinew. Lunge held in one clenched fist an exotic dagger. When Gus examined the panther, he realized the beast wasn't at all a cat but an immense black dog or wolf with blood-red eyes.

"I do love my work." Moiren motioned for the butler to withdraw as if shooing an errant fly. "There are others, if you wish to visit the gallery."

Gus shook his head. He wanted nothing more than to step out of the hot greenhouse and pour a cold beer down his throat.

"No? Pity." He took a few steps closer to Gus. "What I need from you is to pose."

"Pose?" Saul had shown Gus the covers. His first thought had been:

how many boys bought the adventures of *Jove Lunge, Man of Daring* at the newsstands and jerked off to pictures of their hero's physique? Did their mothers find the books hidden beneath the bed and wish their husbands had even a tenth of Jove's stature?

"Yes, yes. One would think, after thirty covers, I would have committed to memory every display of hard muscle and tendon the Man of Daring possessed." Moiren stroked his lips a moment. "But I find it more satisfying to draw from life, capturing the moment."

"It's your spinach."

"An apt bit of jargon," Moiren said and rubbed a nearby leaf as large as Gus's head.

Gus bet the Arrow Collar Man had never had done anything like this. "So I should—"

"Unbutton your shirt, Mr. Lunge."

Gus did so, and when the old shirt fell to his waist, he was mindful that, in his current surroundings, he imitated a flower with drooping white petals. Only, he didn't like thinking of himself as a posy.

"Stretch your arms wide. Curl them in. And … release. Yes, you may well be the best I have seen in some time. I've received such poor offerings lately …." Moiren sighed. No, more like hissed.

"Now, rip your undershirt."

"What?" Gus looked down at the tight cotton taut over his torso. The front was damp with sweat, darkened by his chest hair.

"Rip. That. Undergarment. Now."

Gus shrugged, then took hold of the shirt by the curve by his neck and tore.

A silken leash of saliva linked Moiren's parted jaws. The man's excitement was evident in his trousers.

"Don't you need your paints or something?" Gus asked. He brushed the front of his chest to tease the man.

"Yes, yes." Moiren's voice had softened to an awed whisper. Then the man's trance broke. "Oh, we can't begin painting now. The light fails. Too weak to illuminate the necessary daring. That will happen come morning. Besides, you have yet to meet my other guests."

ONCE OUT OF THE GREENHOUSE, Gus wiped the sweat from his chest with the ripped undershirt, and felt that buttoning his shirt was akin to returning to civilization. The butler took him upstairs, via a groaning staircase and down a dim hallway of closed doors. The butler stopped at the third. "This will be your room for the night. Supper is served within the hour. Proper attire is hanging in the closet." The butler turned a key in the lock. "Do not be late."

Gus anticipated a room decorated like a madame's boudoir, with plenty of pillows, dark furniture, and too much burgundy, like God spilt the wine all over the place, not a room with holes in the plaster walls, a sagging bed that belonged in a flophouse, and by the water bowl and mirror, a pipsqueak in his undershirt, with his suspenders hanging down and a face full of lather. The kid held a straight razor. He could have stepped off the streets of New York, been any of the city gamins, swiping fruit, picking pockets, all the best ways for a dirty squirt to learn the hard lessons life demanded.

"You don't look old enough to shave," Gus said as he threw his travel bag on the bed. Bedsprings groaned. Sleeping on that would be rough.

"And you look like the lost son of Kong." Gus couldn't place the kid's accent but had to admire his moxie, though his eyes were wide, showing nerves. "The Empire State Building is thataway, big fellah." The kid gestured at the window with the razorblade.

Gus strode over to the kid, who retreated in turn until he bumped against the slender table beneath the water bowl. Warm water sloshed them both, but most of it dripped down the kid's scrawny chest.

"W-what, you wanna see my diploma?" the kid asked.

"Who the hell are you?" Gus forced the kid against the faded wallpaper.

"Haven't you ever read a Jove Lunge novel?"

"Lemme guess. You're the shoeblack boy?" Gus grabbed the kid by the neck. The lather made the grip like catching an eel in water, but he didn't want to strangle the kid, just make sure he knew who was tops. The razor dropped from the kid's hand to clatter on the floorboards. "Perhaps you should find another room."

"I-I can't," the kid rasped. "Moiren ...."

"He put you in here?"

The kid nodded. Spittle frothed his pretty lips.

Gus brought his face closer. "Why?"

"Please ...."

Gus released the kid, who collapsed to the floor, where he sputtered a while. Gus kicked the blade out of his reach, not that he looked like he had any spirit in him. "So?"

"Moiren didn't know if you'd rather have kitten or keister."

"So she *is* here." Gus wiped his hands dry on the towel.

The kid shrugged. "The skirt? I just saw her once, when she came in. Real upstage." He rubbed his neck. "Moiren's sedan brought her Tuesday."

"What's your name?"

"Carl. Carl Heim."

Gus nodded. "Okay, Carl, you better clean up. I don't share a bed with bums." *What kind of a job did I get into here?* he thought. Though born in Bayonne, he grew up in Sheepshead Bay, and his first honest dime was made working as a hot walker, leading the sweaty horses around and around the track to cool down. As a man, his first tears came when they turned the tracks into an automobile raceway, all caustic noise and smoke. Not much progress there.

THE DINING ROOM WAS LONG and narrow. Everything was dark wood and shining silverware, which left Gus thinking of a coffin at a funeral. At least a fire roared in the fireplace chasing away some of the chill. Moiren, now dressed in a tuxedo and a Kraut's spiked helmet, sat at the far end of the table.

Gus took a seat at the man's left. He fingered a knife and wondered, if necessary, could he make the throw? He remembered that time in Red Hook when things became a rout ....

"Ah, I see your oldest friend's son has arrived," Moiren said as Carl walked into the room. "Do join us, Timmy."

The kid cleaned up well, some would even call him pretty, with that chestnut hair slicked back and parted down the center.

"Mr. Lunge, I won't ask you to recount your time spent exploring Egypt with the professor, who fell victim to the Blue Pharaoh's sinister death traps. I applaud your kindness at making Timmy your ward and constant companion on your more recent adventures."

"Hope you're luckier than your old man, Timmy," Gus said.

23

Carl took the seat directly across the table from him. He looked anxious.

When she sauntered into the room, Moiren rose from his seat. The photographs of Samantha Kingsford that Saul had shown Gus failed to capture her smolder. Her hair might as well have been coiled flames. She wore a skimpy number that would have given the happiest of married fellahs nervous ideas. Those lips, red and plump, savored rather than breathed the air. She was trouble, all tied up like a kid's Christmas present.

"Miss Samantha, how pleasant you could join us tonight."

"And who is she?" Gus asked. "Jove's squeeze?"

Moiren giggled a moment. "Oh, no. She doesn't have a part to play. At least, not yet. That all depends on you, Mr. Lunge."

"I hope we're having steak. I just adore a good cut of meat." Samantha took the only empty seat, beside Carl, who glowered at her with about as much fondness as a mouse would offer an alley cat.

"I haven't quite decided her role," Moiren said. "She would make an excellent ingénue in distress. Or maybe a temptress playing a risky game. Yes, I think you would all agree—"

"I hope that the dress came free with the perfume." Carl rubbed his nose. She gave him a scathing look in return.

"Well, now that we are all here." Moiren gestured to the butler, who poured red wine for all. "A toast. To *Jove Lunge in the Jungle of Doom*. And to proving Oscar Wilde right. 'Life imitates art far more than art imitates life.'"

Gus brought the wine to his mouth, hesitated a moment, then trusted that the same iron gut owned by his father would keep him safe from mickeys. The wine tasted sour, but Moiren smacked his lips in appreciation. It must have been real expensive, probably from France or Italy but kept dusty down in the cellar for years.

"And what will be the feature course tonight, sir?" asked the butler.

"Mr. Lunge, as the guest of honor, the choice is yours. Would you prefer the game hen—"

Samantha ran a finger around the edge of her wine glass. Gus felt something touch his thigh beneath the table. Her stockinged foot probably.

"—or the capon?"

Carl's face blushed as he looked toward the roaring fire.

Gus realized Moiren wasn't talking food. Was the man testing him?

Could he suspect why Gus was really there or was this simply a game for his amusement? Neither situation sat well with Gus.

"Perhaps he would like a nice prawn, sir." Gus stiffened when the butler's long fingers stroked their way down his back.

"I'll take the capon." Better a familiar dish than one he didn't like prepared ....

"No one ever picks the prawn," the butler said with a heavy sigh and returned to the kitchen.

Samantha wore a bored pout, what reckless, rich girls like to try on when they've been turned down. Carl squirmed, almost as if Gus had grabbed him by the throat again.

AFTER DINNER, THEY FOLLOWED THEIR host into a drafty drawing room decorated—no, Gus decided that wasn't the right word—marred or maybe cursed by his paintings. A Jove Lunge broke the jaw of a masked man with a fierce right hook; another Jove strangled a man in an underground grotto's pool; a dangling Jove clutched the torn canvas of a dirigible covered in Oriental characters; Jove crouched, ready to pounce, behind an idol that resembled a leering squid before which scarlet-robed men prepared to sacrifice a chesty dame. Each painting, each cover, was more reckless, more absurd than the one before it.

Brandy was poured. Moiren struck a match to a pipe, one of those long affairs with reeking tobacco, like a bad fruit pie left too long in the oven.

Samantha sat down on the burgundy sofa inches away from Gus. The butler offered them cigarettes from a silvered case. Samantha reached over Gus's arm to take one.

"So, was it Daddy?" she whispered to him as the butler offered the flame from his lighter.

"What?"

She leaned closer. "I assume it was either Daddy or James who hired you."

Gus began to suspect this wasn't the first time Samantha had strayed. He didn't have a face suited to lying. Or the patience. Playing the palooka served him well.

"Lady, lay off. I don't know what you're talking about. Moiren hired me to be his hamfatter or model or something for the weekend." He glanced in the direction their host had taken Carl, supposedly to show the kid some etchings.

Her full lips had a ready-made pout. "I read those tiresome Jove Lunge books. He rescues the girl at the end. Every time, even when she's no good for him."

"Doesn't sound like Jove's a sharp fellah."

"No. Doesn't. Some girls don't want to be rescued." She blew a stream of bluish gray smoke into his face.

"Isn't always up to the girl. Not when she's featured on the society page," Gus said. "All it does is make men wager on how fast and far they'll run. Like they do the horses on the racing pages."

She frowned. "I'm no break maiden, Mr. Lunge. Unless you have a sedan in your pocket, I'm not going with you back to New York."

The reward for her return was not scratch, but Gus found himself curious why she was there. Couldn't be for the company; Moiren was one brushstroke away from being tossed into the loony bin. No, something was wrong, so he scrapped his original plan of grabbing her, kicking and screaming over his shoulder if he must. And if Saul had taken care of everything, a Packard would be parked a few blocks away.

"So am I the only one here who doesn't appreciate art?" Gus asked.

A bored expression passed over her features. Even though Samantha knew the truth she dismissed him as uninteresting. She seemed not to care if their host knew as well. Was that part of this entire game, or was she daring him to bring her back home? And why, Gus had to wonder, had she run away to Moiren's in the first place?

GUS SAT UP IN BED clad only in his boxers, smoking one of his own cigarettes, not the awful tobacco Moiren offered. He was waiting to see who'd come through the door. Despite his being a gambling man, he wouldn't have wagered. Could be any of the lot.

The knob turned. The door opened a couple inches and the kid peered past the frame.

Maybe I should have played the favorite, Gus thought and motioned for him to come inside.

"Why'd you pick me? You don't seem a queer."

His ma liked to say, *Just 'cause a man's pockets are empty, don't mean he ain't got something to hide.* "Maybe I don't like uppity dames." He tapped a bit of ash over the side of the bed. "Or maybe I like kids that are scared of me."

Carl raised his chin. "I ain't scared."

Gus smirked and patted the edge of the bed. "Then you better get over here."

Carl walked over to the bed and lifted the pack of cigarettes from atop the sheets. He tapped out one and set it between his lips. Then he plucked the lit cigarette from Gus's mouth to set his own smoldering. "You trust Moiren?"

Gus let loose a laugh. "Kid, I don't trust anyone." He stroked Carl's thighs through his trousers. He normally didn't play with rabbits, but the kid was begging for it. "Some don't worry me, though." Moiren though, Gus had to admit, something about the man worried him.

"I asked Moiren why he—"

"Hired me?" Maybe the kid was no chump after all. "What he say?"

"That Jove Lunge had a connection with all his comrades. If Lunge didn't have feelin's for Timothy, then the paintin' would be insincere."

"And pairing us up is supposed to start feelings?"

Gus flicked ash onto the floor. "Like a couple of real nancies."

Carl laughed, but he kept those brown eyes on Gus.

Yeah, begging for it. "I can feel you shaking."

"Am not."

Gus grabbed at the kid's crotch, squeezing tight, not enough to cause pain, but staking his claim. The kid definitely trembled. Moaned a little, too.

"Maybe you don't trust me."

Carl reached out to touch Gus's bare chest. His fingers tugged lightly at the curled hair, squeezed the hard slabs of pectoral muscle. "Honest, you're bigger than I'm used to. I think it would be like wrestling a bear."

Gus let go of the kid's crotch but grabbed his arm and pulled him down into bed, onto him. The springs squealed. "Get ready to make me growl, kid," he muttered before his lips overcame Carl's.

WHILE THE KID SLEPT, GUS slipped out of the bed. He opened his bag. The only change of clothing was a thick black sweater and dark trousers—he did not intend to stay for breakfast. At the bottom of the bag was a pair of brass knuckles. He didn't like guns and had delivered the goods over the last six years without having to resort to one. He slipped the heavy brass into a pocket.

He found the door locked. Not much of a surprise. He could force it easily, but that would be tipping his hand too soon. And he still didn't know where Samantha was staying in the mansion. That left the window.

He glanced back at Carl. If Gus did find Samantha and did throw her into the back of whatever sedan Moiren kept in his garage, where would that leave the kid? A loose end. Saul hated loose ends. Gus wasn't fond of them either. But coming back for the kid would be a mistake. You don't wager on an eased horse.

The window latch turned without effort and Gus stepped out on to the ledge. He was thankful that, though the night air was bitter cold, it lacked a biting wind. He inched along, wary of his step, peering into the other windows he passed, but saw no sign of Samantha.

As he neared one set of eaves, he noticed an old barn a couple hundred feet away from the house. Moonlight showed fresh footprints in the snow leading back and forth. That made Gus curious. He didn't care for the feeling—he wasn't paid to be inquisitive, he was no flatfoot or private dick—but everything about Moiren left him on edge. Not knowing what was in the barn seemed like a mistake. Mugs like him didn't outlive mistakes.

He jumped off the ledge, his landing cracking the semi-frozen surface of the snow, before rolling to his feet. He looked over his shoulder. The mansion remained dark and still.

The barn doors looked ready to collapse inwards. Yet a massive padlock was meant to deter entrance? Gus took hold of the latch. The muscles in his arms strained as he tore it free of the doors, which buckled but didn't fall.

Gus didn't step inside until his eyes adjusted to the darkness. The old scent of hay couldn't disguise a new odor. Musky. An animal, big and furred. His ears caught the rattle of chains from deeper in the barn. Cautious, but curious what the hell Moiren was keeping inside, he crept forward.

A moment before he noticed the crimson eyes high off the ground staring at him, Gus heard the rumble. A growl.

Heavy paws pounded the packed earthen floor of the barn. The heavy chain warned him, and he stumbled back, slamming against the doors, as massive jaws began snapping the air where he stood seconds earlier.

Black wolves aren't supposed to be the size of Packards.

A hand reached in through the cracked doors and pulled Gus back into the open. The shivering butler held a lantern. Moiren, dressed in a heavy fur coat, cradled an elephant gun in his arms. He wore another ridiculous hat, a tricorn, the sort you saw in a Wyeth pirate illustration, and a tremendous smirk.

"So, Mr. Lunge, would you say this night is fit for neither man nor beast?"

"What is that thing?!"

The butler shut the doors behind them.

"A *lusus naturae*. A *fantoccini* created especially for my art." Moiren looked over his shoulder at the house. "Shall we head back, or would you prefer to re-enact something I painted ages ago?"

Gus nodded. He glanced back at the barn and wondered what other horrors Moiren kept under lock and key.

As they trudged through the snow, Moiren rested the rifle against his shoulder.

"Are you a good shot?" Gus asked.

"I've studied the male anatomy all my life. There are entry wounds that will never heal properly, leaving a man crippled for life. I suppose I could aim to be kind, but what sport is that?"

Gus's guts told him that Moiren wasn't boasting. He no longer seemed like the silly fool Gus thought he was. The danger level just made the job a hurdle race. Gus paused and turned back to the barn. "How many Lunges have there been?"

The other two men stopped. The butler began counting on his fingers.

"I mean, have you ever used the same fellah twice?"

Moiren wheezed that awful laugh. "Twice? My good man, I'd be astonished."

"Sir, might I recommend some brandy and Benedictine to warm us?" said the butler.

Gus thought a stiff drink might be the only thing sane waiting for him back at the house.

"Were you frightened?" Moiren asked as he sipped his drink from a flame-warmed snifter.

"I think when you see a wolf the size of a city bus, you've every right to sweat a little."

"Well said. You are not only a man of action—scaling walls and trudging through my backyard tundra, but also a man of sense. Both admirable qualities in a hero."

"Heroes are short-lived."

"Oh, no, Mr. Lunge. You've faced some terrible things—the Hindoo Rahu, Captain Dream and his Zeppelin Marauders, even the Sons of Caqueux in Brittany ... a favorite of mine, I must admit. Just picturing their weaving nooses from the sleeves of condemned criminals leaves me quivering.

"But they're only stories."

"*Only?* Your modesty is a disservice."

"But you know I'm not really this Lunge fellah."

Gus looked at the butler, who gave a tiny nod of disapproval. No, of warning. Too late, because Moiren threw his snifter against the wall.

"You are Jove Lunge!" Moiren ran a hand through his hair, dislodging his tricorn hat. Expressionless, the butler picked it up and brushed the felt with his sleeve. "Don't you see ... I need you to be him."

But Gus didn't see, didn't follow him ... because the edges of his vision had grown cloudy. He looked down at his own glass and fell forward off the chair.

THE HEADACHE, THE AWFUL DRYNESS in his mouth, the reluctance of his eyes to open wide enough to see right, all told Gus he had one mother of a hangover. Only, he couldn't remember having more than a glass of the strong juice that could strip varnish with its fumes. Guess his only inheritance from his old man wasn't proof against something slipped into his drink.

He groaned and rolled over, felt someone warm next to him, cracked his eyes again. Some young guy, dressed like a boy scout, started rubbing Gus's chest and stomach.

"Please tell me you didn't help me cross the street and into a bar."

The kid's hand drifted lower than Gus's waist. "I did my good deed. Twice last night. But today...."

Gus wiped his face with one hand. Despite the way he felt, the kid was managing to wake the rest of him. "Carl, right?"

The kid nodded. Looked even a bit hurt.

"Nice rags. Why are you dressed like that?"

"That butler knocked on the door an hour ago and brought us our costumes for the greenhouse."

"Any chance he brought a cup of joe?" Gus sat up and winced. "Or, even better—a beer?"

All the memories from last night came back to him. Sneaking outside. Seeing the largest mutt in the world chained up in the barn. The mickey in his drink. The butler must have carried his unconscious body back to bed—not that the guy looked like he could handle a sack of potatoes, let alone a dead weight of over two hundred pounds. Maybe he had help.

He wanted to wring Moiren's neck.

Gus looked at the kid. That guileless face smiled at him, even as he stroked Gus's dick. Maybe he wasn't so innocent after all.

"Not now, junior," he said, and took Carl's hand off him. Then he rose out of bed and went over to the washbowl. He dipped his head into the cold water to chase away the fog behind his eyes.

"Go down and tell that bastard I'm not stepping into that vegetable soup he calls a greenhouse without breakfast."

Carl left. A few minutes later, the butler brought into the room a tray with cold meats and warm eggs. More importantly, there was a coffee pot.

"Do get dressed quickly. I've never seen the master so eager to begin painting."

I bet, Gus thought.

THE CLOTHES WERE KHAKI, SHORT-SLEEVED and -legged. A bit snug around the thighs, but Saul's tailor always paled whenever he had to measure him. The hard hat, which the butler insisted be referred to as a pith helmet, felt ridiculous. Gus missed his regular derby.

He followed after the butler on the way to the greenhouse when a *thump!* stopped him. To his right was the drawing room, the door askew. He opened the door and saw Samantha resting atop the divan, one arm stretched down to the floor. A crystal tumbler lay on a damp patch of the Oriental rug.

"I'd watch what you sip here," Gus said, and sat Samantha up. She looked pale, her eyelids fluttering like a caged bird's wings.

He glanced over his shoulder. The butler remained in the doorway; his face turned in the direction of the room's frosty windows. Decorum or lack of interest?

"Mr. Lunge." Samantha rested her head on his shoulder. "Do ... do you want to know my hidden ... my ... my secret?"

Her perfume had faded. Only by being so close against her flushed skin could he catch a trace of its former elegance.

"He promised me ... Moiren said, 'Your father will never forget how I paint you.'" She slipped an arm around his neck, but the gesture seemed not one of seduction but to lean against his chest for strength. "Have you ever felt, that people notice you for all the wrong reasons?"

"Listen, I don't think you know the truth about Moiren's paintings." Gus thought back to the massive beast kept in the barn.

But she nodded, a sloppy, drunken gesture. "I want that cold bastard ... Daddy to be ... haunted."

Gus began to wonder if returning all those girls had been for the best. He'd never failed before. Could deal with Saul's fury at not bringing Samantha back, but he had to confront Moiren first.

The butler cleared his throat. "She's for later, Mr. Lunge. Master Moiren is considering ... well, the unheard of. He thinks you may be worthy of two paintings. You should feel honored."

"Honored?"

The man adjusted his black jacket a moment. "Save the tempest for the greenhouse. As for her—" The butler kicked the fallen glass under the divan. "She'll do for the sequel. *The Last Libation.*"

"Who writes these books, anyway?"

The butler gestured for Gus to return to the hallway.

"Damn it, who writes them?" Gus yelled. He wanted to grab the guy by his monkey suit's lapels and smash him through a wall.

"Don't you know?" When the butler grinned, his scar rippled like a snake across his face.

MOIREN STOOD BY AN EASEL in the heart of the greenhouse. He had traded one odd hat for another, a soft Frenchie number. His worn smock was stained, mostly in shades of an ugly brown. Gus told himself that had to be paint and not dried blood. Bloated and mottled plants surrounded him, and he eyed one's black thorn seeping a fluid clear enough to have been a tear.

"I do hope you both come to appreciate my *Nepenthes rex*. I've spent the last decade cultivating it from seedlings found in an oft overlooked ravine in the Amazon."

"Listen, pal, I think you should know I didn't come here to be your inspiration."

Moiren smirked. "The Marquis once wrote, 'Truth titillates the imagination far less than fiction.'"

"I don't know what your game is—"

"Art. Rooted in suffering is art."

Gus nodded at Carl. "C'mere, kid. Sorry, Moiren, but I think your guests have had enough of your hospitality."

The familiar click of a safety made Gus's head turn. The butler had leveled the elephant gun first at Gus, then at the kid.

"I have painted Lunge with bullet wounds in the past." Moiren lowered his voice, perhaps to sound soothing. "You will all be free to go once I am finished."

Gus cursed. He shouldn't care about some gunsel, but the way Carl looked at him, like a dog fearful it would be kicked to the curb, stopped him from tackling the butler. "Fine."

"Wonderful. Now young Timothy, would you please take a few steps back?"

Carl nodded and slowly shuffled backward until he bumped into the swollen body of one of the plants. Emerald vines snapped around his limbs and he was lifted off the ground.

The tendrils dropped the kid into the gourd belly. They heard the splash and Carl began screaming, in fear, in agony.

"Not yet, Lunge," shouted the butler, who turned the rifle at Gus. An elephant gun would blast a hole through him.

"It's eating him alive!" Adrenaline rushing through his blood, Gus grabbed at several of the twisting vines, his ham-sized fists squeezing sticky fluid from them as he tore them apart.

"Yes, yes. Enzymes and mutualistic insect larvae and all that jazz." Moiren waved a paintbrush in bored annoyance, and then turned back to his canvas. "Now whatever happens, don't move."

POETASTER

NEITHER MIDNIGHT NOR DREARY BUT late on a cold October evening, Atherton James sat before a fire reading a book on legumes. He could not sleep and was relying on both the glass of port and the propensity of Latin within the names and mottoes to lull him. The chair was old, comfortable, cracked leather and would be preferable to tumbled, cold sheets. A knock on the door roused him just as he began nodding off to the illustrations of wisteria—blurs of lavender on the page seeping into darkness. But he stirred at the repeated, redoubled rapping at his front door. He adjusted his robe and his night cap. Secured his slippers. Then, when at the door, he pressed his ear against the dark wood. "Who's there?"

"Teacher!" he heard cry though the grain, the planks, the nails. Only one man referred to James with such a moniker, not altogether untrue, but a career decidedly well past him. He unbolted the lock and allowed the unkempt youth inside his home. It had been ... what, months since he had met Thomas in a tavern and encouraged him to come back to James's quaint Hamilton Street abode? The firelight confined to the hearth barely illuminated any of Thomas; the young man had his overcoat collar drawn high, clutched its edges with white knuckles, and stood hunched in the doorway before stumbling inside. James gestured towards the warmth and light. His own chair, even. "By the fire—"

"No," muttered Thomas. Rather, he shuffled to stand by the dusty bookshelves at the edge of the room and remained in thick shadow. Dampness, either a touch of rain or perhaps sweat, left his thick hair unruly—reminiscent of that striking woodblock print by that Japanese artist whose name James could not recall at present. Oh, it would be found in a volume behind the boy.

"Teacher, somethin' has ... I ain't well." James retrieved his port, held out the glass to Thomas despite the many steps separating them. He did not want to approach closer. Yet. This was all so disturbing, so much more fanciful and fearsome than even the first time he had accepted the handsome young man's offer. Not thirty pieces of silver, no souls were damned— James believed more in illustration than iconography, in the sanctity of the pen over the pulpit. But he had paid, had worried he would be cheated, had been assuaged of all dread when Thomas stripped both of them bare. The sheets had not been cold that night. James had no trouble sleeping that night.

"A drink?" He raised the glass a little higher, so it would catch the light and the boy's attention—James could not be sure where Thomas stared, not while in silhouette—but the boy made no reply. "No? A doctor, then? I could send word. The hospital is not far."

"I heard he went there. Died there."

"Who, my boy? At least come closer. This distance—"

"That author. Poe."

James blinked. Thomas surprised him. They had shared many secrets, much chatter of their pasts, while resting on soft pillows. Thomas had abandoned schooling as soon as he could run fast enough to elude not only instructor but father. This boy should not know the name of any author, least of all a disturbed scribbler who shared his own nightmares with the impressionable public.

"Yes," James said. "I saw the obituary."

Thomas took a tentative step closer. He held out one trembling hand, showing a palm wrapped with a stained handkerchief. "That man bit me 'fore he died."

"What?" Did James not detect a slur to the boy's speech? He put down the port, then approached the boy as a hunter might a wounded boar. "Listen, Thomas. This all sounds like a bad dream. Or a bad bottle of gin. Either way, sleeping it off will do you good."

When he put an arm around the boy's coat, James felt the temblor of shivering reach his own bones. "By the fire, at least." And Thomas let James lead him to the chair and sat down. In the flickering light, as James prodded the dying log with the poker, its stern metal a comfort to his grasp, Thomas's face looked wan, as if he might faint at any moment. The sole fragments of contrast were bits of ebony: sunken eyes, the rash of hair, and the early growth of a mustache above thin lips.

The boy seemed to become aware of the port finally and downed it in one swallow. He wiped his lips with the same hand that dangled the fragile glass. "Needed a theriac."

"Pardon?"

"What?"

"Just that—that word." James dragged over another chair and then took the glass from the boy's weak fingers. "Not something I expect you to know."

Thomas brought his wrapped hand—James saw that the rag was soiled with ruddy brown blotches, which brought bile up his throat—to his chest. "I was there with my ... my *fidus Achates*. No. No, chums. They are chums." Thomas shook his head with the vehemence of a terrier who snatched a rat. "Monday. And we were buying rounds. When he came—walked over to us."

"Who?"

"Poe. Might as well have been H-Hades. No. I don't know who that is. Arghh, Poe. He moved like he was well into his cups already. Drool at the ... at the sides of his mouth. Salivatin' like a mad dog as he asked if he could join us for a drink."

Thomas pulled at his hair. The gesture made his forehead look larger than before in the weak light.

"He had coin, plenty of it, so we agreed. 'What's one more, if he pays?', we always say. I thought I might go blind that night, I drank so much. How did he stay upright? He should have been carried out. To the morgue, for all he drank.

"And then, he starts cursin' and it's words none of us has ever heard. Not even you, Teacher, talked to me like that when I'm fuckin' the hell out of your chute. 'Maggot-pie!' 'Reeky death-token!' 'Withered brabbler on some Plutonian shore!'"

James chuckled. Thomas stopped him by pushing that wounded hand against James's lips.

"No. I-I know what they mean now but I cannot find the humor. Melancholia ... black bile. His bite spread black bile."

"You say he bit you?"

Thomas nodded. "When he became violent, started throwing fists, snapping his great jaws. Bit me on the hand, my chum Willy on the shoulder right down to the bone, nicked the tip of the bartender's thumb in one snap. We let him run off then."

"Perhaps the wound is infected."

"Black bile. I told you." Thomas's other hand pulled at the dark hairs growing on his upper lip. The late hour, the lack of sleep, gave James the impression that those inky strands had become thicker in the short span they had been sitting there.

James cried out when the bell rang and knocking began anew at his door.

"Who is it?" Thomas asked and eyed the door with trepidation.

"I feel that something grim stands at the threshold."

"I'd best see." The knocking grew more violent. James glanced over his shoulder at Thomas before reaching for the latch. A nephew, he would say—the youth was his nephew. He looked old enough, certainly from across the room he might even resemble a man in his late thirties. The poor thing even had bags under his eyes from whatever troubled him so. James confronted his caller, a corpulent man in uniform who steamed from a black-bearded chimney above the chin strap of his official cap.

"Constable Wiggins?"

"Evening, Mister James, sir. Sorry for the intrusion at this hour." The ruddy-faced constable peered past James into the room a moment, then shuffled about as if anxious.

A stout man uneasy at so close to midnight made James all the more tense. He might never sleep this night. "I was just ... well, my nephew is in town and we are up late trading stories—"

"I have stories to tell," shouted Thomas in a pained voice.

"What did he say?"

"Nothing." James stepped closer to the constable and lowered his voice though the chill night air threatened to petrify his tongue. "I-I fear my nephew's had too much drink tonight. You understand ...."

"Of course, sir. That's why I'm calling on you at this hour." He tugged at his beard with a gloved hand. "Seems like much of Baltimore's been hob and nobbing a bit too much tonight—wife won't allow *me* a glass, even the medicinal, as her father was a drunk. And a dago, but still, I married her."

"Constable ...."

"Yes ... well, there's been reports. We've enough burden after that incident at the Chemical Works .... now, these men. Running through the streets." Constable Wiggins glanced in either direction. The street was empty but a sound, perhaps human, did sound out. Perhaps a night bird. "Not niggers or micks, mind you. But good folk have been accosted. Would you believe in Green Mount Cemetery one of these fellows—"

"Well, thank you for the warning," James said and began to shut the door.

"It's a queer night."

"Right you are," said the officer.

"Downright grim," yelled Thomas, who pried the door from James's grip and stepped out into the street. "No, not Grimm. Give me Coleridge's Rime. I want Hoffmann's Doppelgänger." He turned around slowly, his deep-set eyes mournful. "Where am I?"

"Seems a bit off, your nephew."

Teeth almost achatter, James stepped in front of Thomas. "He's ... despondent over a woman."

"Lenore," bemoaned Thomas.

"Odd name."

"She's ... from New Orleans."

"But we loved with a love that was more than love—I and my Annabel Lee."

Officer Wiggins blinked. "I thought his miss was named Lenore."

James offered a weak chuckle. He was freezing in his thin robe, the slippers did little to help, and he only wanted for the policeman—and Thomas—to let him return to comfort of the hearth and his books. "Heh, well, he does find himself in a quandary ...."

The constable raised a hand. "Say no more. Women are the roots of all men's woes. Father would quote scripture on that. 'Ask me never for a dowry or gift, as according to ye the damsel to wife gives unto ...'" He tugged again at his beard. "'Unto …' Well, they're nothing but trouble."

James pressed upon Thomas to head off into the other direction, away from his chamber door. "Uh, that was Genesis?"

"*Batrachomyomachia.*" Thomas yelled. The sound echoed. Or perhaps in the distance it was repeated by other manic male voices.

"I don't remember that book o' the Bible," said Constable Wiggins. "Are you sure he's all right?" The policeman grabbed hold of Thomas by one shoulder. "Messing about with two women. I might think you're crazy."

Thomas turned his eyes to the constable's florid face. Quite without savagery, he leaned forward and bit off much of the constable's nose.

"Fuckin' basta'd," screamed Constable Wiggins as he brought up both hands to stanch the blood. It coursed between the fingers of his gloves, down into his beard.

"Teacher," said Thomas. His chin shone slick with strands of drool as he chewed some, then spoke with a full cheek. "Would you have a pipe of Amontillado?" He chewed some more but could not swallow, spitting out the masticated nose tip on to the dank cobblestones. "I feel a need to rinse my mouth." He turned toward the steps to James's abode.

"Ii 'ose!" When the constable moved his hands away, tufts of his beard came free, collapsing to the ground like clumps of filthy snow. Glimpses of pallid chin were as disturbing as the ravaged beak in the center of the man's face. With a shaking hand, the constable lifted a pistol.

"Thomas," James called. But Thomas seemed not to hear. "Edgar," shouted out James in a fit of insight.

"Yes?" The youth, who had unwrapped the handkerchief around his hand to clean his cheeks and chin, appeared twice as old as when he had stepped through James's chamber door.

He regarded the unsteady aim of the constable. "Ahh, if I may be so bold. At West Point they taught us the proper handling of firearms. You are likely to injure one of us tonight, but not necessarily my person."

"Iim bwinen you to 'ail."

Thomas glanced at James, who mouthed *jail*. Thomas sighed. Not a sigh of resignation. "Impossible. With Nyx smiling down on this city tonight— see, her glowing grin hangs above us mortals—well, I am to explore every crevice, every nook, every cache. What would you know of the beauty of a dying woman? Baltimore knows tonight! What would you say to days of reckoning giving way to nights of vengeance? You know nothing. Teacher, come with me." Distant howls unraveled on the wind. Voices made mad by the wind if they were not mad to begin with. "Teacher, come with us." Thomas wiped the saliva and blood that glistened on his lips. His eyes were heavy lidded like those of a devotee of Mesmer. "A kiss, a nip on the tongue, let me share this newfound appreciation for words, for suffering, and even the most morbid of tastes ... all in a kiss, as once we often shared."

James had not realized how close Thomas was. Then, one of those dark eyes exploded as thunder from a storm held by a fat, bleeding, molting man tore apart much of the right side of Thomas's face. James shrieked at the sight, at the droplets of blood that stained the cuffs of his robe. The constable squeezed shut what remained of his nose and bellowed through his jaws, his voice horribly distorted, "Mister James. Bandages, sir. No. A balm. Like those of Gilead. That will set me right. He was never worth Lenore." James shook his head and ran back into his house. He pushed the door shut, turned the lock, stared at it. He could hear through windows, the spaces where door met lintel, the merry mad shouts of the others afflicted with this ravenous disorder. Though not a young man, he struggled and pushed all the furniture he could against the doors and bare windows. He glimpsed figures running down the street. Dark and pale figures, clutching their high foreheads, gnashing their mouths. Oh, what he would give for some strong, heavy bricks and mortar! That would keep him safe and them out. He needed to seal himself away.

He collapsed back in his chair by the fire. Clasped his hands together to keep them from shaking.

Atherton James was afraid to utter a word. He did not wish to be a man of that crowd.

HE'S SO TENDER

I RECEIVE AN IMMENSE AMOUNT of pleasure from telling my boyfriend Nusur that the vegan hot dog he ordered at this hipster restaurant contains a small amount of human DNA. I love him, I do, but I have been giddy waiting until he finished half the faux wiener. Over the weekend, while he studied anatomy textbooks, I reread old lexicons. My most recent find was "epicaricacy"; I once hoped to score perfect on the verbal portion of the SAT. All for naught, since I dropped out of college after my accident.

Nusur drops the remains of the hot dog on the recyclable paper plate. He stares at his fingertips, covered in a few crumbs of gluten-free roll. On our first date, he made me try lentil burgers.

"Does not," he says.

"A recent food science study found that two percent of hot dogs sold tested positive for *human DNA*. The most damning results were in so-called vegetarian dogs. I think it was two-thirds or three-fourths or some ridiculous number."

With two fingers, I slide his phone closer and closer to me until it falls into my lap.

"You're making this up."

"Would I?" I lift up my vegan wiener, untouched until that moment. It's tepid, but I dunk most of it into my cup of water, saturating the bun, and shove the entire thing into my mouth. My cheek puff, I feel my gag reflex threaten, but I chew and chew as Nusur's face becomes a Dorian Gray print, ugly with disgust.

"It's how the gurgitators eat," I say around a mouthful. "You've never watched the Nathan's Hot Dog Eating Contest? The Wingbowl? That's a Philly tradition." Bits of human-tainted, dyed soy and soaked bun, dissolving before our eyes thanks to my saliva, drop from my mouth like I'm a gorging dragon.

My prince scoots back on his chair, and metal scrapes against the tile and disturbs the surrounding hipster snackers. He can be clumsy, which is ironic, since he's a physiotherapist. He helped me try to walk after the accident. He stood so close behind me as I struggled along the parallel bars. When he gripped my shoulders, I could not stop myself from falling back a little in the hopes he would let me collapse against him. I swooned.

I asked him to take me out for a drink, telling him that a date would make me feel normal. And wasn't that an essential part of therapy? He chuckled but as I was waiting in the parking lot for the shuttle, he brought me a paper cup of coffee he brewed in the breakroom. I told him I wanted more before I finished.

I stir a finger in the water that I'd dunked the hot dog and then drink it down to clear my mouth. "The real question, what I really want to know, is the source of the DNA," I say. "Not the person, but what *part* of the person."

He sips a wheatgrass smoothie. On our first date, he forced me to drink one, telling me that what I put in my body is important. I choked it down to please him. We were at the shore, and he began pushing me along the boardwalk as if I was a tourist in a pushcart and he was the local kid working the summer.

"It's still better than eating an actual, real hot dog. The World Health Organization has classified those as dangerous as tobacco and asbestos. Think about that. *Asbestos.* In your mouth, a clump of toxins creeping down your throat until it sits in your stomach. Dead meat in your belly. Whether it starts rotting first—because all the preservatives make digestion take days—or your stomach acid breaks it down into its component parts, those cancerous fibers are going to paint your colon a cancerous black."

I grin. "You've been inside my colon. Did the tip of your dick turn black?"

He shakes a finger at me. "Rectum. Just behind the sphincter is *your rectum.*"

His father taught medicine in Kabul but in America he drives for Uber. His mother works at a daycare. Nusur has a scar along his torso from an appendectomy. I've traced its length with fingertips and lips and always wonder who cut him open ....

I adore the scene in *Jaws* where the men bond by comparing scars. Cicatrix is another SAT word. The bandaged end of my little finger is so much shorter now, and itches me terribly.

"Perhaps if your skin was browner, you'd have a bigger dick and reach my colon." He's the brownest boy I've ever let fuck me. I'm pink, like pork, the other white meat.

Nusur tugs at the many tiny hairs on his chin. They are curled and bristled like pubes. "And the racist joke happens while we're still eating and not on the ride home. A new record."

I shrug. "It's no fun to make when we're alone." He knows that I'll sometimes say anything to get a rise out of him. I crave that attention.

"How about a Muslim joke? That would be appreciated. Everyone in America likes those." He says this loud enough that we both know the other patrons can hear.

I take hold of his hand, my index finger tapping the spot on the wrist where a paramedic would check for the pulse. "I love you. Like Lawrence of Arabia loved those boys."

"Lawrence of Arabia was raped by the Turks, which left him with ... issues."

He's smarter than me, which makes me anxious, worried that the only way I could truly stimulate him might be by being witty. I know ours is not destined to be a long romance, but I need to be that memorable boyfriend. "Rape, bigotry, cannibalism, we're covering so many taboos and it's not even two p.m. Do I win the Boyfriend-of-the-Year award?"

"Only if you pay for lunch."

I sigh. "Extortion. I do love you."

The first time he went down on me had been the first time he'd ever taken a dick in his mouth. His beautiful teeth scraped the tender skin, especially around my circumcision mark. But I didn't complain: watching his handsome face engulf me left me breathless even as he scratched my glans. I felt as if he were shaving bits of me, swallowing them first before I quickly came.

In seventh grade, my next-door neighbor, a younger boy who had a lazy eye, tried to pierce my ear with a sewing needle, a lighter and a block of ice. He caught a drop of my blood on his thumb and stuck it in his mouth. He was the weird boy on the block. He told me I tasted divine, like a communion wafer. And I swooned.

Nusur leans over to accost the nearest diner, a woman with long hair that shows strata of dyeing, dark and dusty at the ends close to the floor, faded as it Rapunzels up to salt-and-pepper by her scalp. Her shapeless dress cannot decide on just one or two colors but assaults the visible spectrum.

"So, this guy sitting across from me—I just met him on Grindr this morning—tells me that vegan dogs have human DNA in them. I'm wondering if the workers at the vegan dog factory spit into the tofu vats or ...."

The woman wipes her lips with a flimsy napkin that already shows a great deal of lipstick. "You swallow three spiders over a lifetime of sleep, so even if a waiter spits in your food, it can't be worse than that."

Nusur laughs. "You do not swallow spiders—"

The man across from her, who might be her son, might be her younger brother, could be a boyfriend (good for her!), has an upper lip of cappuccino foam. "It's true. I've caught a spider in the house and dropped it onto Astra's lips while she dreamed. I had to push it a little with my fingers but inside it went. And she swallows. She swallows everything."

"Lucky you," I say. "My boy only spits. Though I suppose some of my DNA has to make its way into his gullet."

When Nusur frowns, he denies me his beautiful teeth. He doesn't eat processed sugar. Not a single cavity, whereas my mouth would set off a metal detector. "The Quran forbids cannibalism."

"Sodomy, too. I would imagine sodomizing a Jew would annoy Allah even more."

"You'll so endear yourself to my family with that line."

I want to meet his parents to hear stories of Nusur as a little boy. To see their pride for him. But I worry he'll be done with me before I have the chance.

Nusur stands. I push my chair back an inch from the wooden table. He walks around until he stands behind my wheelchair. He leans down and whispers into my ear, "Of course, ghuls are part of Allah's design. Islam means—"

"Voluntary submission to God." I speak softly, only for him. I understand devotion. After seeing his expression as he unwraps gauze, stripping me bare, and bathes me before he carries me to the bedroom, an expression of being desired more than I have ever realized possible, how could I not yield to him, with every part of me?

THE LETTER THAT DOOMED NOSFERATU

HOW FRUSTRATING TO PEN A serious missive while Emrick seeks to distract me by trifling with his false eye on the bed. I believe he has lost two since I made his acquaintance last month. His current plaything is wooden rather than glass as Emrick shares both my poverty of blood and the dearth of coin brought by treatments for anemia. We met at the sorriest of physicians and he followed me to my flat and has truly yet to leave. I consider him an illness I cannot shake.

He whines a great deal. About his poor fortunes—"Before the war, I would have easily earned a spot in one of my uncle's factories. But I am not meant for a life in steel and fumes." About his urges—"The only relief from boredom is to transgress. Biblically transgress. But does Berlin have a golden calf? No." About his impaired vision—"I think the paint on this orb is poisoning my blood. Some nights I glimpse shapes, see motion …. Not from my good eye, but through this damnable thing."

I groan. "I swear, either put the bauble back in or stuff a kerchief into the damn socket."

"Always scribbling, Tabner. Why you bother to send scraps of paper covered in your inky webs remains a mystery. There are so many men you can speak to face-to-face at a cabaret …."

"Some thoughts are best shared not with beer on the breath …."

"I don't believe I've ever had one of those."

"… and a letter is addressed to an individual. By name. How often do you ever know the name of your indiscretions?"

"They are only indiscretions if I am successful. Your Irish authors would agree with me."

I do not bother arguing that while Wilde would be proud of Emrick's demeanor, LeFanu I suspect would not, and Stoker … well, before I left university, I heard talk that the man perished from the French disease but not before infecting his widow. That poor woman ….

I hear the creak of the old furniture as Emrick leaves the bed and takes the three steps to where I sit by the small writing desk beneath the gap in the wall that once was paned and called a window.

Thankfully he has returned the false eye to its hole. His face would be handsome if I did not often suspect the slatternly thoughts it conceals.

"Let us go out. The sun sets. The cabaret has music. If you are afraid of beer, I will buy us schnapps."

I sigh after staring at the inkwell, nearly as empty as our pockets. "With what? Spielkarten?"

"Charm. I have heard there is a man who stares at many while ordering glass after glass. I aim to captivate him tonight."

"Libertine."

Only as he gets his threadbare coat from the nail on the wall does Emrick think to ask me to whom I'm writing. But because it is a woman, he takes no interest.

THE CABARET MIGHT AS WELL be a photograph with movement and smoke. So much smoke. Colors are muted by what dim light penetrates the hundreds of cigarettes lit in procession. Cigarettes in ebony holders. Cigarettes dangling from ruddy lips. Cigarettes held by nicotine-stained fingertips. Black is fashionable, black is everywhere, black is the only option other than pale skin and shirts and the atmosphere of gray smoke that hides the ceiling.

I cough. Emrick slaps me on the back and I remember the first time he did so, when he was beneath me. A lapse in judgment, an act on the sheets that he read as his papers to stay forevermore in my flat. The sheets, stained by our emissions, were his passport to the country that was my forlorn life.

At the microphone sings a woman in a fine tuxedo. Her hair is short, oiled and dark. Her thick eyebrows and mustache a smear of shoe polish. She gestures to members of the audience during the lyrics of "Heute Nacht oder Nie" as if choosing her partner for later that night:

"Since I once saw you, I cannot withstand you."

Emrick has left my side. I venture to the bar. I lack his talent for looking like a mongrel that will lick rather than bite the hand that feeds it. But then, there are always old men who believe the risk is worth losing a finger. Not that I would snap my jaws. I lack Emrick's insatiable hunger. And there is always someone who needs my talent for translation. My mother believed the only good book was a song book; my father, a lapsed priest, insisted I learn Latin and Italian as he felt Mussolini would end the papacy and I might find work in Trient. I added English to my repertoire because I suspected Hollywood's great producers such as Laemmle or Lasky would do the same.

"Tabner, you must meet this dour fellow I have found to buy us drinks. He shares your obsession with moving pictures." Emrick laughs his coarse and mean-spirited laugh. "And women."

I will admit I prefer the company of a woman's mind to that of a man's. But the rest. Ah, the Creator instilled in me so many needs.

Emrick tugs at my sleeve until I follow him to a table where a single occupant sits with his back to the bar so he may watch the door open to let inside the thirsty, the needy, the lonely.

"You didn't bring me a beer," says the seated man after a swift glance at us. "So much for Berlin's hospitality." His accent suggests one of the outer regions of Germany. He reaches into his vest pocket and pulls out a few coins. "Might as well buy my own. Or three."

Emrick winks at me before rushing back to the bar. "Sit. Your ... friend—I may call him your friend?—tells me you have a fondness for the cinema?"

"For once he tells the truth."

That makes the man laugh. He is not as ugly as most Emrick approaches for money. He is so ordinary. Not a student, not an old man. A bland man, unnoticeable except for the wide-pored skin revealed by being clean-shaven and the gleam of fresh pomade in his hair. He smells a bit rank like he has been traveling a while by train. He's just another man who embarks for the promises of the capital come evening and then returns to mundane life, mundane wife, annoying *kinder*.

He opens a cigarette case. Offers me one but I decline. I am already in his debt for a drink. More and he might expect my ass. "I try to see as many motion pictures as I can. Who is your favorite director?"

A very unordinary question, as most filmgoers I meet in bars such as this seem to care only for the faces on the screen rather than the hidden masters. "Lang. Wiene—"

Acrid smoke roses from his cigarette. "Ahh, how that Jew's *Caligari* enthralled me. Mesmerism. I often wonder if the large screen is not some great eye that beguiles us all."

Emrick returns with three beers in small glasses. I am sure he will forget to return to the stranger whatever coin remained after such an extravagant purchase.

"You think we're all somnambulists in our seats ready for the dictates of the director?"

The man shrugs. "It is not as far-fetched as *Der Janus-Kopf*? I think Murnau's art is mired in phantasmagoria."

I may set my glass down too hard. Emrick kicks me under the table. The stranger flicks ash in the tiny puddle of spilt beer near my glass. "To enjoy Wiene and reject Murnau is like ...." I, who regularly pen letters to men and women around the world, find myself at a loss for words. Kind words. Civil words.

The stranger chuckles. "But his latest is of a Nachzehrer."

"A film based upon a brilliant novel."

"What book is this?"

Emrick finishes the little beer at the bottom of his glass. By his expression, I know It tastes terribly sour. "Must we talk of books? Haven't we had enough imagination to dull the sense? Look, friend—"

"The name is Kürten." I hear iron in our benefactor's clipped speech.

"Kurt, dear friend, after drink and smoke, the next delectation is the firm thighs of a woman. I happen to know several that would smother you with perfumed tits, a skilled mouth—"

"It is Kürten. And are you not both Hinterlanders?"

I stand. I have been called much worse but never in one of our cabarets.

"Sit, sit, Tabner. There is no shame in the truth." Emrick turns back to this schwein. "Who better a woman to trust than a man who has no claim to any of her lips?"

"There are brothels a plenty in Berlin. Some might even take your money," I say.

Kürten turns his head to look at the singer who is in the midst of "Kann Ich dafür?" "I am curious what it would be like to bed a woman who wears a man's clothes to feel whole. Is she still warm inside?"

"Very warm," Emrick says in a low voice. His pose, his tone, everything about him so disgusts me that I resolve to never speak to, or touch, him again.

"I would be amenable to that." Kürten doesn't look away from the singer. And so he misses what I see next: Emrick nodding before his expression changes. As if half his face, the hemisphere housing his false eye, is overtaken with temblors. He lifts a hand and covers the other side, as if blinding, masking, much of his face. He gasps, which brings the stranger's attention, but by then Emrick has stumbled out of his chair and headed back to the bar.

Kürten chuckles, a sound without any warmth or mirth. "I offend. I am from only Düsseldorf. There I catch curs and bitches. Dogs. You are obviously well-read. Come, sit back, enlighten a man. Perhaps change his ways?"

I glance over my shoulder at Emrick, who is demanding in a pained voice drink from the bartender. Something is terribly wrong.

"Sit," the stranger commands. I do, because I feel troubled and do not know what I should do or where I should go next. Or is it that his voice has a weight to it that enhances the gravity's pull on my body, which now feels weak like an infant? I suspect he must talk to his wife and *kinder* in such a beguiling tone. And they do not refuse him, either. "This book you mentioned? It is good? What is its title?"

"*Dracula.*" I leave unsaid my preference for the original title: *The Un-Dead*. He nods but says, "I have not heard of it."

"You are only from Düsseldorf."

He smiles and reaches over to my glass, which has sat abandoned, not quite emptied. He downs its contents. I notice an ugly rash along one side of his neck. "Tell me more. I assume that there are beautiful women in this book. And cruelty."

"It was written by an Irishman. A man named Stoker. A nosferatu travels to England and preys upon several women."

"English women? Already I can see this is foolish. Why would he like the taste of their blood? Our woman are strong."

"Then you'll be pleased to hear that Murnau's film is set in Germany," I say. "It premieres tonight."

"I had not planned on staying so long in Berlin but if you are attending I could be your guest."

I feel shame color my face. "I-I cannot afford such a ticket. It is a gala affair at the Primus-Palast." Besides, the thought of spending more time in this man's presence is unthinkable.

He gestures with his cigarette at the singer, as if marking one of her notes in the air. She smiles at him. It is her trade.

"Perhaps you are only afraid to be proven wrong about Murnau. Meet me tonight at this Primus-Palast. I shall pay your ticket. I always feel generous after ...." Kürten stands and walks toward the singer. "After," I hear him echo.

I join Emrick at the bar. In the short span from last I saw him, he has managed to drink himself into a near-stupor. When he realizes I am standing by his elbow, he blinks his authentic eye at me. The other stares wide. "Nothing," he mutters. "Not you, but around him, they all float."

"What are you talking about? Do you enjoy introducing me to these reprobates? If you wish to be my Wotton, at least surround us with beauty."

"He was surrounded." In trying to nod towards the strange man named Kürten, Emrick nearly falls. "They're all around him. They all float."

I hold him steady by the shoulders. Once, I might have kissed him. His mouth is slightly agape with a strand of schnapps-scented saliva connecting those lips. I'm disgusted that part of me still finds him appealing. "Make sense."

He writhes, shaking loose of my grip. Then his fingers reach for his wooden eye and in front of everyone who took to staring at his raised voice and physical antics, he plucks it loose of the socket. "This. This sees girls, young girls, old girls, so many girls ... they're like those flickering actors you adore so much. Not on a screen, but they're all around him. M-Mutes. Mute, flickering girls." He then vomits.

Cringing at the stench, a hand covering my mouth and nose to prevent myself from getting sick, I turn to where Kürten was talking to the singer. I see neither.

I help Emrick back to my flat. He is in a stupor as I strip him bare and clean him. The sight of him so helpless is overpowering, and fucking his ass serves as a panacea for the day's worries. For I have decided I must accompany Kürten this evening.

I have read too many tales of the macabre to resist the chance to see phantoms, whether they are real and haunt Kürten or cinematic and haunt Murnau. To be among the elite few that attend the premier of *Nosferatu* ... would both impress and endear myself to Frau Stoker and Frau Holland. Their opinions of me are all that matter these sorry days.

I RENT SOMETHING SUITABLE, SOMETHING not so old as to embarrass me, arguably wasting my very last mark. If I am even a day late in returning it to the Jew, he will demand a pound of flesh.

Kürten waits for me. He has also changed his clothes but they seem ill-fitting. I watch as he smokes another cigarette. Parallel scratches to the left side of his nose are raw. I think of the singer's hands. Had she worn kid gloves? And then I realize that his suit is the same as hers.

Neither can I repress a shudder nor is he bothered by the reaction.

"I am pleased you came," he says to me. "I thought you might not."

"Even my ilk has occasion for boldness."

He nods in mock appreciation.

My free hand accepts the ticket from him. I see beneath his fingernails is filth. How much time must pass before something so vital as blood becomes raff? Less than a day? An hour? Beneath his shirt are there more scars, more ruddy daubs?

My other hand remains in the pocket of my trousers as my fingers encompass the wooden eye. I aim in the darkness of the theater to lift Emrick's eye to one of my own, squint and peer through it as if it weren't wood but a camera obscura. I need to know if Emrick did see phantom girls. The false eye has grown quite warm from my touch. I can feel it is not a perfect sphere. I wondered along the walk to the Primus-Palast from what tree had it been carved and by whom? Both of my favorite correspondents married storytellers with a penchant for the gruesome and romantic. What would their men have conceived of mute ghosts? Alas, I am not so creative but I am anxious, the trait common men possess instead of imagination.

"How do you handle your wife?" I ask.

"Hmm?"

"Does she know about these ... trysts of yours?"

A better question I should ask is why I am fascinated rather than frightened. My insides twist, yes, I sense a shiver ready to take hold of my entire body as I remember the words Emrick muttered— Mute girls, *even as I fucked him I think the thrust forced his torso to work like a bellows and he moaned* Mute girls *repeatedly. Or have I developed an imagination finally after reading so much Stoker and Wilde?* —tonight my eagerness to discover the truth behind Emrick's claims rivals my anticipation for Murnau's film. If there is a threat from Kürten, I am inured to it.

"No," he says. "Perhaps one day. I am not so different from a somnambulist; something sleeps within me, even while I work or eat or talk with you. It stirs now and then. I imagine we all stretch and kick when we sleep. A pillow is lost to the floor. The sheets tangled. I have grown to love tangling sheets." Both his hands become fists, crushing his own ticket, dropping the cigarette.

"But this beast still sleeps?"

"Beast?" He blinks at me, as if the word has no meaning. Or the wrong meaning. I repeat the word, more for myself, in Latin and English and then German again.

"Does an expectant mother think the child up her prune a beast? No, they all think it's the next messiah."

I DOUBT I SHALL EVER set foot in a more lush building than our movie palaces and the Primus-Palast might be the finest I visit. My eyes welcome the rows of electric chandeliers on the plastered ceiling that brighten everyone's countenance except my benefactor's. My lungs breathe in a not-unpleasant blend of colognes and perfumes and expensive tobaccos. My feet are comforted by soft carpeting.

A lad grins and takes our ticket and an usher smiles and leads us to our seats. Both wear crimson uniforms with shiny buttons and gold epaulets. Germany has proud soldiers once more, but they escort through rows that can house more than a thousand eager patrons rather than perish in muddy trenches that hide many bloated corpses.

We are in a row not too far from the large orchestra and the stage, which could swallow the cabaret as Leviathan did Jonah, and the velvet curtains that frame the massive screen would be coveted by Emrick as ideal swaddling for every illicit act imaginable.

Thoughts of Emrick brings thoughts of ghosts, as does the death of all light in the theater and the commencement of the orchestra. Overhead, an amber ray pierces the darkness. Some in the audience gasp. There are always those who have yet to experience a motion picture. Even I am captivated by the science, which I could easily believe to be occult rather than optic.

The first title card—*Account of the mass death in Wisborg in the year 1838, by ? ? ?*—has Kürten asking me in a whisper, "Where is Wisborg?" It is not in Transylvania, I am sure.

I slip the false eye from my trousers and roll it back and forth between my hands. The audience is captivated by the film. And when I read the card, *Travel fast, travel well, my friend, to the land of ghosts,* I can only think that Murnau himself is whispering to me to look through this wooden lens for the real Kürten.

I rest my head against my hand so as to bring up the orb in as surreptitious a manner as possible. At first I see nothing. Not until I shut the unobstructed eye. Then, I glimpse a pale fluid dripping down Kürten's forehead into his eyes. Immediately the temple beside the false eye erupts in pain; I think I am not meant to see such things, that flesh and blood are allergic to spirit. But I persevere and the fluid coalesces into small hands that are hiding —no, blocking, they are trying to blind—the man's eyesight. But if he can feel their presence, he does not react. Rather, he is chuckling as he watches. At what, I dare not look, because gaunt, white arms and shoulders are coming into view for me.

"Now that is a beast," Kürten says and nudges me. The miraculous— or accursed—eye drops from my grasp. I am blind for several moments. I cannot see his face or that of anyone else in the theater. Not until I turn to the screen do I see the beast he fancies.

No Dracula. No white-maned wolf of a man, no immortal lean-and-hungry Cassius. Stoker would choke at the sight of this vampire, who is an ignoble and bald rat which has discovered how to dress in funereal garb, walk about on two long legs and taunt the audience with its talons. This is not a noble predator but a carrion-eater. Why does Germany persist in its adoration for the Great War's losses?

I look away. Kürten smirks. I wince at this expression and search the crowd. Surely they must all be aghast, horrified. And by the flickering light above and beyond us, I do see their eyes wide, their hands covering their mouths to keep silent. But too I see the occasional sardonic grin, the rare flush of a man or woman who looks more ready to rejoice than scream. When Orlok arrives by ghost ship in Wisborg, he easily, comically escapes the notice of the incompetent bureaucrats who seek the cause for the plague. I hear Kürten mutter, "All too true," and I am sure this man is all-too familiar with avoiding the attention of authorities.

I yearn to flee the darkened theater but even the lamps outside would be little comfort. I need sunlight. That is what is supposed to kill Orlok. But what will sunlight do to men like Kürten other than let them notice that the filth under their nails is dried blood?

And the final scenes, of Orlok's true death and the mourning of a man over the still body of a beautiful woman? Am I the only one in the theater who realizes this is but a weak reflection of life, that monsters are not confined to nitrate but are seated unbeknownst beside us?

Kürten's grasp on my arm is forceful; but he claims it is only a courtesy to allow the slower members of the audience to clear the row first.

"I am in your debt," he says. "Murnau is no charlatan but a black magician."

"I must admit I am less than pleased your opinion has changed."

He laughs and gestures for us to leave. Together. I find that he matches my quickened pace with skill.

"She was like all the others, you know?"

I assume wrongly that he means Orlok's victim.

"Once shed of those manful trappings, she was soft. Too soft. When they are delicate, it is too easy to silence them. I dread the day I hear a woman speak in a motion picture. It would ruin the fantasy. Do you know the folk tale of Patient Grizzel? She is the ideal woman because she will not raise her voice to her husband."

He has led me to one of the many alleyways that turn Berlin into a warren. I lean against a stone wall. Gas lamps flicker in the distance. His shadow looms large, reminiscent of one scene from the film, of Orlok ascending a staircase.

"I think I shall head to the train station now," Kürten says. "No need to thank me for this treat. I don't think you want to thank me."

"You trust my silence?"

"I trust your terror. I think you will linger a while at this very spot until you are sure I am far away. Perhaps you will listen until you can no longer hear my footsteps. Then I suspect you will drink whatever you can afford or beg so that you might forget me.

"But you won't." He steps back, letting shadows fall over him. "You will go tomorrow to that very cabaret and hope, like a sick suitor, that the singer will appear. And when she doesn't, will you curse Murnau? Because I have drank deep of your adoration for that man, and now the bottle is either sour or empty."

I ADMIT THAT HE SPOKE the truth. But before I venture to see if the cabaret can ever again offer me some measure of comfort, I take a circuitous route back to my flat. My mood is dour. How many performances of *Nosferatu* will there be? How many will be comforted, even inspired by it? Despite it being a travesty of Stoker's brilliant novel, caricatures are favored by the uneducated more than the original.

Emrick snores. One eyelid lies limp against the vacant socket.

At my tiny desk, I notice the unfinished letter to Frau Stoker. Has she any idea what has been done to her husband's legacy? I think back to the film and wonder if *Dracula* was even credited as its inspiration. If not, then some salvation might be achieved.

I crumple the letter. Tomorrow I will sell her husband's book. I care not what I'm offered; I cannot look at its cover or pages without thinking of the many authentic beasts hiding within men.

I take the pen to my last, virgin sheet of paper and slow my handwriting to ensure there will be no error, no spill of precious ink. If Frau Stoker does reward me for alerting her to Murnau's poaching, I shall purchase Emrick a fine eye fashioned from glass by a real artisan. And we will drink and never talk of books or phantasmagoria again.

As I sign my name and gently blow upon the ink to dry it, the corners of my eyes tear. I think in the darker corners of the room, the ones the candle at my desk cannot reach, shapes are applauding because they cannot speak and what I write must serve as their only voice.

UNWELCOME BOYS

DAWN MIGHT BE ONLY A coming thought at this hour, and the near-deserted parking lot of the bus station is quiet enough to lull Terry back to sleep, if not for the hot coffee he's been drinking from the thermos that rests on the bench seat between him and his older brother. The vintage Chevy pickup has been nursed back to health every year by their father but lacks air conditioning, so the windows are down. Summertime has crept into the asphalt and wants to make the air dance. Zeke's arm hangs out the driver's side as if this would prevent the smoke from his cigarette to enter the cab.

Terry wants a sip of coffee, even if it smells burnt, but Zeke filled his mug from the gas station and, on Terry's anxious, empty stomach, the stuff would haunt him for hours and hours. He begins to chew the hard peppermint candy he's made last for more than ten minutes. He once lasted almost twenty.

Last week Terry read online that raising the body's temperature helps burn calories faster, and to lose another five pounds he's been wearing layers for days; he doesn't dress so much as conceal himself every day. Sweat trickles underneath the three t-shirts he has on, making them sticky beneath the hooded sweatshirt, its lettering faded, sleeves too short and neck too small, but it's survived the years since his father wore it in high school, and Terry thinks of it as a charm of sorts, as precious as the gold wrestling medallion that floats on the perspiration from his neck.

The out-of-town bus to Massachusetts is due in a half hour.

Zeke flicks ash before bringing the smoke to his mouth. "Don't get a seat near the back." The cigarette's end glows orange. "Those last four rows ... you'll smell nothing but piss the whole trip."

The trip will take over thirty hours, but the bus fare is so much cheaper than an airplane ticket, that Terry is willing to endure any hardship to attend wrestling camp at the academy.

"You're likely the only one arriving by bus," Zeke says as he dumps what was left in his mug onto the lot.

Terry shrugs. "They probably have limos."

"The rich drive Ducatis and Land Rovers." Zeke grinds the butt into the old ash tray, which gives the dashboard a serious metallic underbite.

The price tag for the camp is a ridiculous sum. Zeke whistled when Terry told him how much, and his brother asked if he wouldn't be happier with buying a car for the same money. "I'll find you something with a V8 and dual exhausts. It will roar, and all the boys at your school will rubberneck. They'd beg you for a ride. Bet you'd like that."

But a fast car won't help Terry one day escape the meagerness of Archbold, Ohio.

How could Zeke understand when he stumbled after graduation? And keeps stumbling? He is almost five years older than Terry, who has noticed the same gray stubble all over Zeke's lips and chin that their father possesses, the exact color of cigarette ash. His brother scratches beneath the frayed brim of his Toledo Rockets cap, which hides dark hair in sore need of a trim.

"I got you a going-away present." Zeke gestures at Terry's shins. "Look beneath your seat."

Terry reaches an arm down, searching beneath the cracked vinyl, until he feels something crinkly. He retrieves the brown paper bag, which tears apart as he opens it. A sleek box of condoms lands in his lap.

Terry punches Zeke in the meaty part of his upper arm.

His brother raises his hands in a gesture that would profess innocence if not for the smirk on his face. "I'm looking out for you—stop hitting me! You're going to be hundreds of miles from Archbold. *Get some strange.*"

Terry has never even kissed another guy. He doesn't dare think of such things because the idea is both terrifying and tremendous, like how he imagines gunpowder would smell. "I can't—"

"Why not? Those other boys won't know you. Or see you after these next two weeks."

Zeke dates the empty-eyed girls who work the early-morning shifts at the counters of the local Sunoco or Brupp's Donuts. His attraction seems dependent on a lack of ambition as much as a curvaceous pair of hips.

"They might. There's Nationals—"

Zeke scoffs as he fills his coffee cup and spills some onto his overalls. "Aiming high, little brother?"

Terry groans as his brother's taunt scratches him, but, though honed, there's no blood drawn.

"Don't be afraid." Zeke's finger jabs the cigarette lighter.

Terry winces, even as he tells Zeke, "I'm not afraid." Though, he wonders if he might be. He tells himself that the only way to avoid being the *gay kid* at school is to remain hidden in plain sight. His family knows, so he's not really in the closet, just … biding his time. Wrestling will lead to a scholarship, which will lead to a smart life someplace other than Archbold. If his teammates know he found guys hot, they would get weird, and the locker room would be hostile. And then he would start losing on the mat, ruining any chance to escape.

If he can deny himself food during much of the year, one more temptation won't be a challenge. "Fine. I'll take them." He shoves the condoms into his backpack. He doesn't want to argue about his life, and he can throw them away later.

As he walks through the parking lot, over the cracked asphalt, his brother shouts at his back, "You know how to use them, right?"

Terry answers by turning around and flipping him off with both hands held high.

THE BUS WHEEZES, THE AIR inside so warm he suspects it's stale. Wanting anonymity, the other passengers turn away from Terry as he moves down the aisle to a pair of empty seats in the middle of the bus. He drops his bags onto one seat, then curls up on the other, beside the window. He empties one pocket for his cell phone and cellophane-wrapped peppermint candies. Having refused Zeke's offer of breakfast, Terry's feels hollow with hunger.

His friends have been eating like locusts ever since wrestling season ended, but because of camp, Terry has not strayed from his strict diet. He wanted to lose another three pounds before the start of camp. He wrestles at 132 but would impress the Academy's coaches at 126. He doesn't trust the old scale at home; it creaks worse than the springs of the second-hand sofa bed in the basement, and the needle of the dial drifts back and forth underneath scratched glass before settling on a number. 128.

Back in March, right after Terry's last match as a sophomore, his coach pulled him aside and astonished him with the news that he'd recommended him for the Academy's summer camp. The Academy's wrestling program won conference titles. Because admission was highly competitive, the chances of them accepting Terry weren't great, and Coach recommended that Terry consider camps closer to home to hone his skills.

He kept his daydreams small enough that they could be worried over in under an hour, often as he ran in the early morning or just before bed. Sweating felt like proof he deserved something good; losing another pound an achievement he could own, a win on the board.

As the calendar promised warmer days, his friends began to chatter about summer jobs they might find, what they'd spend their paychecks on, what might happen with the girls they met on the warmer nights. And Terry kept working out, burning off thoughts of spending his summer pretending that a few dollars and coaxed kisses tasting of off-berry lip balm would satisfy.

The email arrived the week of final exams. He told his mother there was no way his head could retain algebraic relationships or transform boundaries when it echoed with words like *unfortunately* and *waiting list*. On the sofa at night, he would glance away from whatever textbook rested in his arm and watch his father putter around the kitchen—after he washed the dishes he would embark on an hour or so of repairs, ones so minor that maybe the squeaks of a cabinet, the shudder of a drawer, the cough of the pipes, might be imagined. Terry tried to summon the words needed to ask his father if there was any work at the garage, but the question was a chunk of gristly meat he should have either chewed or spit out but instead he swallowed.

He missed the phone call. He was jogging through Roll Park and ignored the tremble. As he walked home, he listened to the message. A gruff voice told him that one of the wrestlers enrolled at the camp was too sick to attend and, if Terry wanted the spot, he should call back immediately. His lungs suddenly would not clutch the air as his fingers fumbled. He anticipated no one would answer, or worse, he'd be told that it was too late, they asked another boy. Four rings felt like forty. But the same gruff voice answered, and Terry was offered his second chance.

By the time he reached his block, he realized he couldn't afford the camp fees or even the bus fare to and from Western Massachusetts. He was thankful his parents didn't let him spiral into despair and promised him they'd find the money for him to go. And that haunted him, because it was no secret that there wasn't much to go around.

Terry emptied his savings account, its meager number intended for college tuition, but success on the mat would pay for higher education. He sold his second-hand gaming system to a friend, then his bike. He pawned downtown the gold chain on which he wore the St. Sebastian medallion, given to him by his grandfather after a winning-freshman season.

There are only thirty-three carbs in each peppermint, yet Terry slowly works the twisted ends of the cellophane with the anticipation of opening a Christmas cracker. During the season, on bus rides after matches, the coach threw miniature chocolate bars at the team. Whether a reward for a win or solace for a loss, the candy thrilled the boys, who competed amongst themselves to be the one with still a visible sliver of chocolate on his tongue by the time the bus reached Archbold High.

With the peppermint tucked into one cheek, earphones in, Terry strokes his phone awake and starts watching videos of district tournaments. His idol, "Bo-bo" Ogbonna, last wrestled 131 for Virginia Tech, All-American honors, came second at the NCAA championship, a maestro of the ankle pick. But Ogbonna started off wrestling for a small school outside of Cleveland, a poor district. And Terry loves to watch Bo-bo's signing-day video, almost as much as the guy's matches, because Bo-bo could not look happier or more handsome, hair in twists, as he announces becoming a future Hokie.

In stolen moments, certain that none of his friends or schoolmates are looking over his shoulder, Terry will watch that video from Bo-bo's junior year of high school, when the camera caught a pronounced outline of an erection right after a match. But even that indulgence, and the requisite ten minutes of frantic jerking and subsequent wiping himself clean with whatever t-shirt was on hand, left him guilty. And on the bus, well, he didn't dare.

THE BRAKES HUFF AND GROAN, the chassis shakes, and Terry wakes with a neck both stiff from awkward sleep and slick with perspiration.

The air outside is heavy with humidity. He paces the sidewalk outside the station as he speaks to the woman who answered the camp's phone line. She is kind yet rushed, as if she would rather be elsewhere. "Someone is coming for you," she says. "I think he has a Jeep."

A topless Jeep does pull up beside the curb a few minutes later. The driver stands up in the car. He's young and plucks at the front at his sweaty, school t-shirt, as a signal, before telling Terry to hop inside.

He introduces himself as one of the camp's proctors. Darren. Or maybe it's Dean. He talks fast, drives fast. "You're a buckeye, right? How was the ride? Varsity?" Terry's answers might be stolen to the wind.

"I don't think there's another tucker who's come from so far away." The Jeep's tires squeal as he makes a quick right turn off the main road onto a serene, residential street, with tall trees shading houses so old that many have little wooden signs proclaiming historic significance, but the words are lost in passing.

From the street, the sight of the Academy, a medley of stately stone and brick buildings, decorated with thick columns and plenty of dark green ivy, releases adrenaline into Terry's bloodstream. He takes a picture as the driver sets Terry's bags into the pavement; his mother loves to look at online listings of million-dollar homes.

A green-and-white banner with the words *Welcome! You're Better Boys* hangs across the widest building, yards away from where they parked. Terry wonders if it's New England slang, and asks the driver, who shrugs.

"I think that's some kind of self-help program. The Academy hosts a lot of summer programs." He tips his head toward the kids walking through the tall, wooden doors of the nearest building, most of whom don't look like wrestlers. "Right through there is registration. Someone will check you in, then show you where you'll be rooming. This afternoon is orientation. And then a barbecue, so I hope you're hungry. See you soon."

With his bags at his feet, Terry lingers at the base of the stone steps until he sees unkempt boys with impetigo scars and gym shorts climbing them, and only then does he heft his things and walk inside.

As TERRY WALKS ALONG THE stretch of asphalt that his paper map shows runs through campus, he overtakes another boy, roughly the same height but definitely a 185, who glances up from his map with a confused expression.

"Where did they put you?"

"Uhh, Zeddies."

That earns a grin. "Me too."

"It should be by the baseball field," Terry says, pointing.

The heavy-set boy picks up his duffle bag and eyes Terry's sweatshirt. "You're a Bluestreak? I'm an Icebox. Maine, of course."

"Ohio."

He pumps Terry's hand. "Abner."

They walk together, and Terry listens as Abner tells him about the differences between huckleberries and blueberries.

Inside their dorm, almost a dozen boys layer the noise, spoken or sung, and beats and belongings are dropped. Terry finds his room on the second floor and feels relief he does not to have to share it with Abner or anyone else. The simplicity and tidiness—a twin bed against the far wall, a tiny desk and chair, a low dresser topped with a stack of clean sheets and bedding—is so bland as to be comforting. He's pleased to see there's no air conditioning unit in the window; if the nights are hot, he might sweat enough at night to lose another pound.

He empties his bag onto the desk, then smooths his rumpled clothing before refolding each and arranging them in the dresser drawers. The box of condoms didn't travel well, stuffed as it was into his backpack; the sides have caved in, and the slick squares have spilled out. He lifts one and squeezes it, trying to discern the texture, and deciding it vaguely gelatinous and likely disgusting to the touch. He worries that sex might be distasteful. The few times he watched porn on his phone, it looked more awkward and pained than any of the tussles on the mat.

He sweeps the condoms from across the desk and into the trash bin, then snaps a picture for Zeke. He sits on the unmade bed for several minutes, struggling over composing the text message, before finally feeling witty with *Found the right hole for these*.

Then he strips layer by layer; he's been wearing those clothes for almost two days straight, and the resulting funk has saturated everything. His veteran nose isn't offended by the smell—more intrigued at how his armpits hold a scent like brown mustard left out on a picnic table for several sunny days.

With a bar of chalky soap in hand and a coarse towel around his waist, Terry walks down the hall, mindful of the other open doors that offer glimpses of the boys settling into their spaces.

The communal bathroom lacks a door, and as he looks for the showers, Terry catches sight of gangly legs on the floor tiles before a wide-open toilet stall. The rest of the scrawny boy in a ribbed tank and briefs kneels at a toilet with one hand clutching the front edge of the seat. He glances over his shoulder at Terry, and his face is pasty, with dark crescents beneath both eyes. "I'm alright," he says, with an almost cheery tone, before sticking two fingers back into his mouth, deep to the throat.

Even with the water flowing from the showerhead and over his head, Terry still hears the gagging sounds. They only cease when he is nearly finished drying off. He walks around the corner to find the boy at one of the sinks, brushing his teeth.

Terry thinks, *He's a mindful bullfinch after all that purging*, though the boy is so small, probably not even 100 pounds, that Terry doubts he's a wrestler. The boy's expression as he squints at his reflection, before adding even more toothpaste to the brush, demands thick glasses atop his nose.

"Are you okay?"

The boy spits fragrant minty froth into the swirling water. "Yep." He opens his mouth wide, and again leans so close to the mirror, he could rub noses with his reflection. Then he turns to Terry. "Can you see anything at the back of my mouth?"

Terry hesitates, then leans down. He sees nothing out of the ordinary. "Uh. No, looks fine."

Then the boy scoops up water from the faucet's stream and smacks it into his mouth.

"How'd you get the scar?" he mumbles with dripping lips.

Terry looks down at the crooked pale line, running from his sternum down to that spot just above one wing of the iliac furrow, where he often pinches to see how much body fat he has.

"That's from when I squeezed through a fence and caught a nail."

"You're one of the wrestlers." The boy's tone is flat, as if he's disappointed. He taps his toothbrush against the faucet as if it were a xylophone bar. "I saw the scar and thought, maybe you're here for the Better Boys Meet-up. Lots of us think maybe cutting would help, but no one I know has ever risked it." The plastic side of the toothbrush smacks down one last time. "You go too shallow and the unwelcome can't get out. Too deep and ..." He makes a raspy sound, widens his eyes, and pantomimes a gushing stomach wound. "Parents lose their shit when they see blood."

SMOKE RISING FROM THE BARBECUE grill flavors the July air and leaves Terry salivating like a mad dog. He spits on the manicured grass to clear his mouth, and eyes the lines of boys—he sees that Abner is amongst them—with their paper plates eager to reach tables laden with platters of charred beef and veggie burgers, mounds of potato salad and coleslaw in bowls, stacked ears of corn. His stomach is growling, or maybe it's begging, so he scoops baked beans onto his plate, adds a cob, and hopes the fiber will leave him feeling full. Abner is less picky.

Terry chooses a patch of grass at the edge of the crowd, where he'll only see a few of the boys chewing, that queasy and constant applause for the cooks. He's already sitting down when Abner waves at him.

Then, Terry's peripheral vision tags a shaggy-haired boy running from the pavement over the lawn, right toward him, a collision about to happen. But at the last moment, the boy swerves and bounds, missing him, and in that brief close call, Terry can read the words on the boy's sleeveless t-shirt: *Bottom Man*. The askew rainbow beneath the lettering could only be drawn by a distracted child. The boy's wide mouth sucks in a breath before uttering a rushed apology.

Terry notices how the boy's dirty blond bangs bounce as he steps lively through the crowd. Like so many wrestlers, especially short ones, the boy's body is all inverted triangle and stout limbs. He's twitchy, always in motion, even when his bare feet are planted on the soft grass.

Terry waits for the crowd to start sneering and braying at that t-shirt. But other than a few nudges and whispers, most of the wrestlers greet the shaggy-haired boy with back slaps and pound hugs as he moves among them to find a spot to sit. The nonchalance amazes Terry: back in Fulton County that shirt would not be tolerated.

Terry throws out his stained paper plate in the recycle bin without noticing that he's eaten everything edible, the cob savaged without so much as a surviving kernel.

In the middle of the wrestling coach's welcome speech, Abner leans in and whispers to Terry, "I heard if this guy thinks you're good, they'll take you."

Terry scowls. "What?"

"The Academy. All this is the finest. And you come here…" Abner snickers. "You're made."

DARREN WAKES THE WRESTLERS WITH quick raps to their doors. Downstairs, he warns them that he won't be their alarm clocks again.

Abner yawns as if in the dentist chair and plods along beside Terry.

"You meet any of those Better Boys?"

"Yeah."

"So weird. A guy at the barbeque told me he saw one of them reach into the compost bins. And eat trash."

Terry shrugs. He feels a cranky edge building inside of him; he didn't sleep well, as he imagined what it might take to impress the staff.

The Academy's dining hall feels it's almost a reverent space, with polished floorboards, columns rising to the high ceiling, with round tables and chairs instead of pews. Terry thinks his entire house might fit into this banquet space.

As he dawdles in line for the breakfast buffet, he counts maybe fifty or so other kids in the hall. He then glares at the trays heated underneath by flickering Sterno tins. The sight of grease glistening like dewdrops on sausage links and bacon strips leaves him queasy, and he moves past them and the tureen of hashed potatoes. He scoops out a small lump of scrambled eggs onto his plate, adds some fruit, before straying off to a table close to the immense windows.

He eats quickly because he does not want to linger—it seems idle. Abner leads other wrestlers to the table. The sound of chair legs squealing as they are dragged across the floor, makes Terry wince.

He glares at Abner and the piebald-necked boy that sits between them. Then he notices the two glasses of milk on each of their trays, and stares at the pale wave sloshing as Abner's elbow jostles his plate. Back home, there's no real milk—Terry's father has a stomach ulcer so there's only pricey almond milk, which tastes off to Terry and never truly cold no matter how far back in the fridge he shoves the carton.

"Where'd you get that?" he asks, leveling his fork at their glasses.

Piebald gestures over his shoulder at the open doorways to the kitchen.

The scrawny kid from the dorm's bathroom stands at the milk dispenser, but acts as if Terry isn't standing behind him while he fills a couple glasses.

Everyone's greedy here, Terry thinks as he lifts a glass from the boy's tray. "Thanks," he mutters before taking a long gulp.

He has never tasted anything so foul. He shakes his head, and blinks his eyes. His tongue feels coated with something bitter and sour, yet cloying with flavors he cannot place.

"What ... what was—"

The kid giggles and tells Terry what was in the glass *before* he added milk.

Terry's throat trembles. He starts gagging. He's thankful he's only a few steps away from a conveyor belt loaded with plastic bins heaped with dirty plates. He throws up into a tipped cereal bowl. A kitchen worker starts shouting.

Ashamed and his nose filled with the acrid stench of recovered eggs, Terry asks the kid, "Why?" He thinks he can still taste what was in the glass. "Why the fuck would you—?"

His answer is first a shrug and then, with a smirk, "It wasn't for you."

THE PROCTORS LEAD THE TWENTY-FIVE campers from the dining hall out into the sunlight, then walk them into another of the Academy's fancy buildings. They skirt around a massive brass seal inlaid in the floor, and pass a floor-to-ceiling glass cabinet filled with trophies and silver cups, proof that victory gleams.

Terry imagines for a moment what it must like to go to a school that promises everything. He comes close to touching the glass of the trophy case but won't dare leave his fingerprints where they're not earned.

The practice space disappoints. A narrow area with tall wooden bleachers along one wall, and the entire floor is a scuffed green mat with circles. The signs proclaiming victory hanging over one doorway look old, individual plastic letters pegged into boards, despite announcing a classmate who won the New England Championship last year.

The shaggy-haired boy is among the proctors, but he's at the other end of the gym, thankfully, as he's wearing another handmade, trimmed shirt, that taunts Terry with not only the faded lettering proclaiming *High Crotch Takedown Champ* but glimpses of hairy armpits and muscled arms.

All the boys are restless, some fidgeting with mouth-guards, others working the kinks out of shoulders, a few stretching and chewing on their shirt collars. One meets Terry's gaze and begins to shake and gurgle, mock vomiting, which makes the skin on Terry's face burn. He will need to face that boy, drop him fast, before Terry's marked.

The morning sessions on technique begins as the coaches ask the proctors to demonstrate leg defenses. Terry chews on a sliver of fingernail as he watches. Some of the moves are familiar, but he's determined to master each and every one. These are the secrets that he hopes will give him the edge.

The campers pair off to practice those moves. Terry matches himself with the mocking boy, who is so eager to razz him that he's rushed and sloppy. Terry swoops in, toppling him in seconds. His adrenaline is a more preferable fuel than the breakfast he upchucked, and he's pleased as he repeats his wins even as he starts feeling puffed out and seeing the room slip sideways a little, so he has to lean against the bleachers to catch a breath.

The head coach makes his rounds. A long-faced man with thick-lidded eyes that make him look sleepy, or perhaps bored, even as he starts calling out names. "Patulski, come here."

With a headful of anxiety, Terry hopes for a grunt or two of praise, but the coach instead lifts up Terry's chin to examine his face, then rubs a calloused thumb hard against his forehead. "Early to be winded. You cutting weight?"

The question is unexpected, and before Terry can stammer an answer, the man is looking down at his clipboard and sucking on his teeth. "You look lighter than 132."

"My coach thought I should drop down." It's a lie, but one Terry feels won't be checked.

"He ever bump you up?"

Terry nods. Occasionally, his coach back home would ask him to step up, wrestle heavier guys, when the roster was down a man. One teammate was out with mono for almost a month. "A couple times."

The coach yells, "Thatcher!" When the shaggy-haired boy comes trotting over, Terry's mood sinks. He notices how the boy's neck is so shiny with sweat. He's a good three inches shorter than Terry, but his wide chest remains intimidating.

The boy holds out a hand. Terry is a moment late in meeting the grip.

"Patulski here normally wrestles at 132, has ninety-six wins. Scale's shy right now, but I think he could go 138. Work with him the next couple of days and tell me if I'm wrong."

Terry's flummoxed. He's never felt comfortable wrestling when bumped. He understands his body, how it works head-to-toe at 132, and knows he's sleeker at whatever weight he is now. The weight classes aren't arbitrary, they don't bend because of this man's whim ... they are essential to the sport. They're holy for Terry because they're numbers, which neither conceal nor judge. "But I'm doing fine ..." *Ninety-six wins.*

The coach isn't even looking at him. Instead, he's hunched over so he can whisper into Thatcher's ear. It's the kind of move that makes any athlete cringe on the inside, even as he struggles to pretend indifference. Thatcher nods and that damp hair gets in his eyes for the moment.

The coach finally remembers Terry exists, because he glances at him before returning to his clipboard. "Patulski, don't let this guy goat you." And then he's off to the next group.

Dispirited, Terry follows Thatcher to his new squad; he can feel their eyes weighing him, their internal scales far less kind than the ones that measure pounds rather than pins.

"Patulski, since you're standing, you can help me teach these lucky socks," Thatcher says with a gesture. "Take starting position."

Terry takes his stance, squaring his hips. He can feel his blood rush in anticipation, because he knows that, at any moment, the older boy will rush at his legs, throwing both arms around a knee to try and topple Terry.

The best countermove, what all the campers have been watching over and over, is to grab the opponent's head when he nears your waist and thrust it down. But the maneuver has become fraught; Terry knows that Thatcher's face has to be brought oh so close to his crotch—he thinks of his hands gripping the thick hair, sliding down the boy's sweaty neck—and even with the athletic cup he's wearing, a fresh helping of blood buoyed on his rising heartbeat is making this terribly uncomfortable.

Not since seventh grade has Terry felt as if he might pop a boner at any moment while wrestling. In middle school, it was the thing he dreaded most, even when it was clear that many of the other boys similarly worried; hormones and grabbing and friction often left awful evidence in the front of a guy's singlet. Even worse that, despite misery supposedly liking company, seeing other boys like that only made things worse. And soon, every shower Terry took in the locker room, whether after gym class or a meet, was a cold one that left him shivering. He prides himself now in no longer staring at other guys, not in the hallways of school, not during a lull in a lesson or when a class is forced into silent focus by a pop quiz. Not when stripping of clothes, changing into uniforms, and certainly not in the team showers.

He tells himself often to shove any and all desire deep into his viscera, a wondrous word he discovered while paging through a Scrabble dictionary one family game night. Every guy that he's wrestled has been straight and would be shocked, sickened really, if they ever learned what Terry sometimes wanted to do with them. But Thatcher, he's unlike any of the boys Terry faced across the mat. Thatcher is intimidating, in fact, with his unexpected … Terry is unsure of the appropriate word. Outness. Thatcher's shirt alone distracts Terry every time he looks at the older boy. When he's not noticing the boy's flushed neckline, his muscled arms, his gray gym shorts ….

And as Thatcher lunges forward, grabbing a hold of his knee, Terry finds himself caught in the moment. Gone is muscle memory and instinct. When his fingers sink through the bangs, though they are damp with sweat, it's like flint meeting steel, and the sparks of kinesthesia ignite his palm, his wrist, his entire arm becomes alive and eager to abandon direction and press

Thatcher's face to his body rather than toward the mat under their feet. Terry then hesitates, in effect surrendering, and the older boy easily topples him. And having Thatcher atop him should be impermissible, but the heated heaviness pressing against his torso is so welcomed by Terry's every nerve. He thinks that his moves now are not to flip the older boy off him but evade getting pinned only to prolong the frottage.

He loses.

Again and again, because the older boy refuses to leave Terry, despite his flushed face, and stumbles and falls. Even when the roles are reversed, Terry finds himself too disconcerted by the nearness of Thatcher's crotch, the inviting open space between fabric and thigh, and reads the contours in the hopes of divining what lays beneath the polyester blend. He takes so long to lunge that it's pathetic, and Thatcher wastes no time in trapping Terry again beneath him. Terry breathes in Thatcher's scent, redolent from their friction; it reminds him of sawdust but sweet enough that Terry breathes deep to ensure the memory is locked away in his lungs as much as his mind.

Thatcher doesn't roll off Terry right away. No, he brings his lips close to Terry's ear, the breath causing him to stiffen. "Next time, keep your breakfast down," the older boy whispers.

Terry's bite on his mouth guard should cleave it, as he his limbs burn before shoving the older boy off him.

OUTSIDE, THE ACADEMY'S GROUNDS HAVE been taken over by small boys sitting in circles on the grass. Like the workings of a massive clock, one would spring to his feet and shout, "I'm better not because of him but 'cause I raised almost a thousand dollars for my local foodbank," before leveling an arm across the space to choose another, who stands with a cry of "I'm better ... not because of him ... and I know all the state capitals," and then another. "I'm better than him because I can speak English and Korean (fingers are held aloft for counting) and a little Tagalong—that's Filipino."

"What's that about?" says one of the heavyweights.

Abner and Piebald start telling them all how weird the Better Boys are. "And they think they have a demon inside of them."

"What?" "So cray." "You're shittin' us."

The boy Terry dropped hard shakes his head. "There's one in my dorm. He stopped me yesterday as I was unpacking. Asked me if I knew the Heimlich. I looked at him, an' he's not choking, so I told him I did. And he offered me twenty dollars to do it there in *my* room."

Piebald grimaces. "Maybe he should ask that fag proctor?"

Terry finds himself suddenly grinning, comforted to hear the hate he has been waiting to seep out of the cracks and into the open, and all his fears about ever coming out are reaffirmed.

TERRY HEARS A "HEY YOU," AND instinctively stops. From an open doorway, the scrawny kid steps out into the dorm hallway.

"Sorry about the milk."

"It's okay."

"What's your name? I'm Goshen. It's biblical."

Then the kid grabs Terry's arm and starts pulling, making Terry stumble into the room. Terry fears he's suddenly going to be asked to do something like the Heimlich, but the kid gestures toward his desk, which is covered in torn scraps of paper and marker pens.

"They told us to write messages and put them on the walls and under our pillow." Goshen rolls his eyes and in a higher pitch says, "I'm normal and that's okay and special too." He bounces once on the bed. "But you, you could write something—"

"Me?"

Goshen nods and hands him a pen. "Just put down your *feelings*. Don't hold back."

Terry scrawls on a scrap *Leave me alone.*

Goshen lifts the paper close to his face and reads it aloud and laughs. Then he shoves it into his mouth and starts trying to swallow without chewing. As he backs away, Terry thinks he hears the kid mumbling, "I like that."

ON THURSDAY NIGHT A MOVIE is shown outside on a white sheet fastened to the brick wall of a building, one probably older than Terry's grandparents. The campers rest on the lawn and watch *Paradise Alley*. They erupt in laughter, especially the scene where one guy, acting tough, rips off his sleeve in a show of force before arm-wrestling the unfortunately nicknamed "Kid Salami." That sobriquet is uttered again and again by the boys with more raw emotion than the actors managed.

Thatcher is relaxing near the film projector. He's tossing popcorn into the air, and a couple of the other proctors try to snatch the kernels while they're aloft, but most are snapped by Thatcher's quick jaws. Terry is instantly envious of the one guy who is a moment too late and gets his fingertip bitten.

WALKING BACK FROM THE EARLY afternoon session, Abner is still buoyant from pinning Darren. "My slide-by, that's my spell, my *qualifier*." He slaps his chest. "Think Millburn noticed?"

"Maybe." Terry looks at Abner's frame and tries not to see its bulk.

"It's so nice here. Where I'm from ... Perkins is like a ghost town. It's so small. And I hate it so much. Not that Bath's much better, but that's where we'll end up. Mom and me."

"I won't last in a small town," Terry says.

Tanned workers in green shirts are hauling large rocks and bags of briquettes, creating a fire pit in the center of one lawn, and some of the Better Boys watch them toil from underneath the comfort of a shady tree in the mulch.

"I heard they wander around the school at night."

Goshen lifts an arm and waves at Terry, who sees the dour kid beside him make a clenched fist and punch Goshen in the stomach.

Terry runs across the grass. Goshen is on the ground, clutching his middle. Terry bends down to help Goshen stand. Abner has grabbed the arm of the boy who struck Goshen, and he looks almost eager to shake the kid until something breaks.

"Why the hell did you do that?" Terry yells at the kid.

He seems genuinely startled at their anger. "I'm helping him hork," he whines and struggles. "We do it all the time."

One of the groundskeepers asks Goshen if he's okay or does he need to go to the infirmary, but he shakes his head no while he heaves and coughs. He looks at Terry. "Would you walk me back to my room?"

Abner mouths *Don't* and shakes his head.

But Terry sees how rattled Goshen seems and can't bring himself to refuse.

"What about this one?" Abner eyes the kid as if he might bite. The grounds-keeper is walking off, clearly not wanting to be involved further. "Terry?"

Goshen hugs himself as he walks.

"You all really think there's something ... bad inside you?" Terry asks him. Goshen rasps, "I know it."

"But how do you know? Have you been X-rayed?" Terry glances in the direction of the gymnasium. Without his phone, he isn't sure of the time. The Academy has a large bell that sounds off the hours, but he can't remember if it's closer to three or four o'clock. He doesn't want to miss the next session.

"Of course. They've done everything." Goshen holds the door behind him, clearly wanting Terry to follow after. "I've been through an MRI. They've pushed scopes down my throat. Even up my butt—" His eyes roll. "And that's about as fun as you imagine. None of the doctors saw *him*. And that's because he—all the unwelcomes—they hide really well."

At the stairwell, Goshen frowns. "I know what you're thinking. I can see it on your face. That look—everyone always gives us that look. But none of us are crazy. Science hasn't caught up to us yet. Einstein predicted black holes without knowing exactly what they were. Took years for them to solve the mystery." He starts climbing. "And that's how it will be for us."

"And this unwelcome ...."

"He's my twin. I think. There's these stories about one twin eating the other while in the womb. Something like that happened." Goshen looks down at Terry from the landing. "I don't need you to understand. You can't. And it's awful. I always feel as if there's this terrible person inside me."

"And they sent you here?"

"My parents are so afraid." Goshen opens his mouth and lowers some fingers down and down for a moment, gagging a little. "They see us dropping fishing hooks on dental floss down our throat." He lifts his shirt. "Or marking our sides with X's to know where to cut. And they think we want to hurt ourselves. Send us to therapy. I don't have self-esteem issues, I just want *him* out of me. But he won't come up." There are tears in his eyes, as if talking about the unwelcome is more painful than the sucker punch.

"Have you ever tried fasting? Lot of us—lots of us wrestlers—it's how we stay in control. We keep weight. Staying hungry gives me focus."

Goshen puts his palms over his stomach, perhaps over the spot where he was struck. "He gets angry when I don't eat. He starts twisting my insides."

Terry shrugs. He suspects he'll be late for instruction. He puts a hand on the doorknob. "Look, I once saw this on TV … a guy came back from vacationing in South America He ended up with this parasite from eating something from a street vendor. I think it was a worm wrapped around like organs so they didn't want to operate. Instead, they prevented him from eating anything. They didn't even give him one of those IVs. But they put a tray with a juicy steak right beside his head. Oh, and they strapped him down, so he couldn't reach it. After a couple of days, the worm inside him was so hungry that it started to crawl up and out his mouth to take a bite of that steak. They caught it, and pulled it out, like it was as long as a snake. But that saved him."

"No shit?"

Goshen's expression shows so much desperation, that Terry feels suddenly guilty for offering crackpot advice. "Total truth."

TONIGHT THERE IS A COOKOUT, and the boys surround the fire pit and dare one another to just lean a little closer to the flames with their metal forks, skewered with hot dogs or stuffed hot peppers. Before the trays of marshmallows and graham crackers, chocolate and bananas, are consumed for dessert, the proctors take turns entertaining the campers: one plays on an acoustic guitar, another quizzes them on moves with ridiculous names (the Chicken Wing, the Pannage Drag) and throws out folded space blankets as prizes. The sound of crinkling mylar echoes the crackling flames.

Thatcher takes his turn on the piece of lawn that serves as center stage. Though barefoot as usual, he has on a dark-green hoodie with the Academy's name across the chest and green-checkered shorts. He lifts up one of the tennis balls he's holding. "I don't know what you guys like to do when wrestling season is over." He starts throwing out the balls into the waiting hands of the audience. "Me, I needed something easy." He puts two fingers into his wide mouth and whistles. The balls fly back, and he starts catching and hurling each into the air. "For me, it's juggling."

The boys applaud. He throws the tennis balls back into the crowd, then leans forward into a brief bow. "Now, I need a volunteer."

So many arms rise, so many voices shout out. But none are Terry, who is bewildered when he hears Thatcher call his name. He stands there, wanting to be truculent and stay put, but Abner pushes him forward, and he has no choice.

"Now my daring assistant," he gestures at Terry a moment, "and I will be trying for a record. Three balls. One hot dog. With mustard." He begins rubbing his palms together. "When I count down from five, you will throw first the balls, one at a time, to Terry. Throw them underhand please, I don't want to mess either of our good looks." He turns to Terry. "And you'll repeat my number as you toss me each item."

Someone shouts, "He must like you, Terry. He trusts you with his balls," and Terry winces.

"All of you need to be careful handling my balls," Thatcher, which raises hoots and laughter.

"Five!" And Terry catches the first ball, pausing long enough to call out the number. And so goes four and three.

"Now the mustard. Two!" The squeeze bottle spins as it arcs throw the air. Terry catches it just before it hits the ground.

"Make sure it's open, Terry," Thatcher calls out.

Terry twists the spout and almost forgets to shout two before he throws it at Thatcher. The older boy grasps it hard and a brief stream of bright yellow mustard erupts. Before it falls on Thatcher's arm, the bottle joins the balls in their circuit. "And the hot dog?"

One of the proctors asks, "Bun or no bun?"

Thatcher is keeping his eyes on the balls he has aloft. "What do you think, Terry?"

Terry glances in the direction of the fire. He imagines Thatcher singeing his fingers, fumbling. The one Terry forced himself to eat had tasted as if rolled in charcoal. "Bun."

Thatcher nods. "Bun that tubesteak! And now ... one!"

With great flourish, the proctor standing at the front of the audience slides a hot dog off a fork, cradles it in the bun, before soft-pitching the whole thing underhand to Terry.

"Wait for it … I need more speed." The balls, the mustard, blur as they arc.

Piebald, it has to be Piebald because of that bellow, yells, "Give him your wiener, Terry."

Terry feels as though someone slapped him in the face. Worse, much of the crowd has rallied around this as a chant, arms are raised.

He could drop the hot dog, like a mike, tell them all to fuck off before stomping off, but he knows that will castigate him as the most despicable things, a poor sport. So he weakly says, "One," and throws the hot dog at Thatcher, who catches it easily and takes a bite. The crowd roars, then watches as Thatcher spins everything, squirting mustard into his mouth (though much lands on his face and chin) before taking a second bite. By the time he has messily shoved the rest of the hot dog into his open mouth, the cheers are a force that Thatcher feels at his back, and he can hear the applause as he walks away.

THE NEXT DAY TERRY DOESN'T utter a word to anyone. He leaves the dorm early, doesn't join the wrestlers on their morning run, but ventures into the fitness center to uses the rowing machines while wearing ear phones. He chooses a partner at practice to avoid being forced into volunteering with Thatcher. At meals he takes his tray outside and sits on the hot, sun-soaked stones of the dining hall's front steps.

Several of the Better Boys are also outside and skipping lunch; Terry watches them surround Goshen, who looks listless stretched atop one of the many, low ornamental walls, his shirt raised to his sternum. One of his arms hangs over the side, the twitching fingers the only sign of life, as one after another of the boys bends down to press an ear to the bottom of a plastic cup they move across his bare belly, which barely rises and falls. But if any of these boys actually hear an unwelcome lurking inside Goshen, none react.

THE SWEAT FROM THE AFTERNOON'S training and the long run Terry took to avoid dinner makes Terry's clothing feel like a swollen second skin that must be scraped off before getting rancid. He wants to collapse on the bed, close his eyes until tomorrow. His hand grips the door handle to his room when he hears his name called out. He turns his head, and a spike of anger drives into his exhaustion when he sees Thatcher down the hallway trotting toward him. The proctor has probably come to chew him out over missing another meal.

Thatcher's a bit out of breath, with flushed patches on his cheeks, when he reaches Terry. And his hands remain behind his back. "I know the first few days here are kinda intense and can sometimes suck."

"Yeah."

"I'm sorry you've had it rough. And I've made things worse. What happened the other night ... I chose you because I thought you'd have fun helping me." He holds up a wrapped ice cream bar in each hand. "I stole these from the dining hall freezer."

Terry's surprise doesn't allow much more than a murmured "Thanks," and a hesitation before taking the peace offering. Thatcher doesn't know that Terry hasn't eaten ice cream in over five years. His grandpa would take him to the local ice cream parlor most Wednesdays after school. And then his mother sat Terry down and told her father was not a well man, and that he has something called diabetes and should never eat anything sweet, definitely not sundaes or banana splits, which would make him very sick. But when his grandfather picked him up in the afternoon as he liked to do, Terry couldn't bring himself to refuse to a trip to the ice cream parlor. That must have been an early autumn afternoon, and they split a dish with five scoops of pumpkin pie ice cream, topped with crushed graham crackers and whipped cream dusted with cinnamon. And Terry kept it a secret, but when he learned days later that his grandpa was taken to the hospital, the truth came out on a torrent of tears. The doctors told this family that grandpa would likely lose his left foot but maybe they could save the rest of his leg. Holding the popsicle stick now is a cruel reminder of holding grandpa's cane a moment as he tries to sit down comfortably.

The first bite of ice cream is like wading into frigid water, and the sugar stings his teeth.

Thatcher rips off his wrapper, and rivulets of chocolate ice cream pour onto his hand; he contorts to lick clean his knuckles and fingers. But the attempt is doomed, and the streaks left on the older boy's nose and chin make Terry laugh. And then Thatcher lifts up the hem of his shirt to wipe at his face, and allows the secret landscape of his abdominals, all pale skin, taut muscle, and small hairs, to be seen.

Terry's staring is interrupted when a large dollop of melted ice cream tumbles down his sleeve. He can feel the cold lick his wrist and forearm. "Damn it!"

"Here." Thatcher takes what's left of the bar from Terry's grip, allowing him to swipe the door handle. Once inside his dorm room, Terry tugs off the many shirts up and over his head. Arms still wrapped in damp cotton, he turns around to see Thatcher drop his green cinch bag on the floor, then throw the wrappers and messy popsicle sticks into the trash. But then the older boy looks hard down at the plastic bin before picking it up.

"That's a lot of condoms to bring to camp." Thatcher's chuckling deepens. "You either *just* realized there's no girls here ..." He stops speaking a moment because the laughter is making him breathless. "... or you took one look at the *boys* and thought, 'Naaaah.'"

"No, no, no," tumbles out of Terry's mouth as his body trembles; Thatcher might as well have reached inside of Terry and plucked at his spine.

Thatcher's grin implodes. He drops the bin and takes two steps closer, reaching for Terry's bundled forearms. "Hey, hey, I didn't mean to ..." He swallows. "I'm sorry. I'm a total asshole."

"Please don't tell. Please don't." Terry's face must be so hot that the tears burn off before reaching his chin. His exposed skin has heated his body, making the scar across him incandescent like a lit sparkler.

Thatcher's eyes widen with understanding. "Oh shit. I didn't know." He lets go of Terry so he can push aside the thick bangs from off his forehead, briefly exposing his own scar, a tiny divot at the hairline. Thatcher looks as if he might also start shaking. "I swear I won't say a thing."

Terry struggles to free his arms from their burden. "Can you go?"

But Thatcher begins pulling at the tangled sleeves on Terry's forearms. "I don't know if you should be alone right now. You're really upset." A bared arm is revealed to be streaked with chocolate.

"I-I need ... I-I just want a shower."

Thatcher forces his fingers through Terry's grip. "Listen, I am going out in the hall, and I am going to call the staff and let them know you're staying in your room tonight—"

Terry's head shudders. "Don't say—"

"I'll *only* tell them you're homesick. Nothing else." Thatcher squeezes his hand. "They know it happens, and they'll want me to stay with you a while. I'll order pizza. And if you want to talk, we can talk, or just sit here and eat, but I really don't want to leave you like this."

And Terry realizes he has little choice but to nod, though he sighs in relief when Thatcher steps out of the room. If only the door could be locked. He collapses on the bed, and covers his head with his arm, smelling the ice cream on his skin. Thatcher's excuse for him isn't a lie; he wishes he was back home in Archbold now. But it's so far away. Even if he begged Zeke to drive all night, all day, to come for him—and he is sure that Zeke would make the drive—leaving the Academy now wouldn't make things better. He would come home as a failure, knowing what his family did to get him there, to bring him home. He doesn't know if he can trust Thatcher, but he also doesn't have a choice; Terry will let him stay as long as he has to, make polite conversation, but he has no appetite to eat, no need to unburden. Not with all the hurt and fear percolating his insides.

He leaves his room wearing a towel and clutching a bar of soap. He has on underneath clean briefs because he cannot bring himself to be almost naked, not when Thatcher sits on the hallway floor almost within reach. Under water that hasn't warmed yet, Terry rushes to shower. He grips the cake of soap with whitened knuckles. Will its slight perfume wash away the grime that humiliation has left on his skin? He scrubs hard. After a quick rinse, he dresses within the stall, stopping when he hears what might be footsteps. Fear worries him: Thatcher might suddenly slide the curtain open and step inside.

And yet, there's a sour bubble of disappointment in his throat when he finds that he is alone in the bathroom. He swallows it down when he sees the older boy hasn't moved from the hallway.

"Okay, you're accounted for," Thatcher says as he lowers his phone. "And pizza's on its way."

Terry nods. He needs more clothes on to feel safe, though he worries it's not Thatcher who is threatening but his own infatuation for the boy. Despite only a bit of breeze coming in from the open window, he reaches for the single, long-sleeved shirt he brought, and blue jeans and socks.

TERRY WATCHES WITH A SICK fascination as Thatcher, sitting on the floor by the dresser, eats. Slices are devoured in ever larger bites, and tomato sauce and grease seeping from a topping of extra cheese repeatedly leaves the older boy's lips red and shiny, reminiscent of the girls Zeke dates. Thatcher wipes his mouth and chin with the back of a hand, that hand then wiped on his gym shorts, and the shirt between them (*Sweat Equality Not Sweat Equity*) is apparently well-familiar with the exchange as there are ghosts of stains turning its front into a faded map.

Lying on the bed helps Terry keep his distance both from pizza and Thatcher. Terry wants to ask Thatcher how he dodges scorn. There must be some cheat code that gives him this total abandon so he can flaunt being gay without losing the respect of teammates and coaches. How did he learn to time even winks and smirks?—he's doing so right now, being charming even though ten seconds earlier he was lifting a nasty clot of mozzarella to his jaws, heedless of what dripped down on his collar. This wink and smirk are so perfect, that Terry finds himself grinding a growing erection into the mattress.

But why would Thatcher ever share the secret? So he asks the boy something lame.

"This is my third year here, but first as proctor," Thatcher says. "A little pocket change earned while keeping my edge during summertime. Not a bad thing. Better than last year: I was a farmhand."

Terry laughs. "I bussed tables at this restaurant. Blanche's. Thursday nights were the worst, because they offered veterans this dish for only five bucks." He starts searching on his phone until he finds the right picture. He tosses it to Thatcher. "Creamed beef on toast."

Thatcher's eyes widen. "Oh, I don't know what that is ..." He's laughing. "... but it looks as lewd as it sounds."

"It's awful. And those nights the whole place is filled with seniors asking for their 'SOS'—a few of 'em don't mind asking the waitresses for shit-on-a-shingle. By the time I clean up tables, the plates are slimy, and the smell of that sauce ... ugh, I swear people eat disgusting things."

"Sometimes." Thatcher wipes his face more thoroughly. "I think you don't like to eat."

Terry looks down at the floor. "Not much, no." The less he says on the matter, while remaining honest, the better.

"If they don't see you eating more, Millburn will get worried."

Terry shrugs. The man's not his *real* coach.

"Maybe I'll get worried, too."

"I guess I'm all sorts of trouble for you."

"You are." The floorboards creak a little as Thatcher crawls over to the side of the bed so he can look up at Terry. "Do you parents know?"

"Me being gay? Yeah. The summer before middle school, I spent a lot of time getting in trouble in my neighborhood. Behind my house is a culvert, leads back and forth through the block. And at one end there's a property that's fenced off. It's an old fence, mostly crooked posts and beams. There were plenty of shrubs planted because they had this outdoor pool. And one day, I'm walking past and catch a glimpse ... brothers, both varsity football, going down this slide into the pool."

"Mmmhmm," Thatcher murmurs.

Terry sighs. He hasn't told this to anyone before, and he wonders what happened to his resolve. "And that night, all I could think about was the sight of those boys, all shiny and wet, slipping down that slide together. And I went back. Every day that week. And I would sneak onto their property, going a little bit closer each time. Until I was hiding in the bushes."

"And?"

"They saw me. And chased me, of course. I ran back to the edge of their yard, to the fence. And because I was so scared, I was careless. Clumsy. I went through rather than over, and a rusty nail on the post just ripped me apart. I remember being covered in blood. And the brothers must have taken one look at this kid bleeding and shrieking, and they ran."

"Damn."

"I don't remember running home, but I guess I did. And the blood dripped all over the kitchen floor. My mother and Zeke were home, and they kept asking me what happened, but I didn't want to tell them. Ended up going to the emergency room and getting plenty of stitches, tetanus shot. And when my father came ... I couldn't tell him everything, but I said enough. And he must have gone to the boys' house. And whatever he told them …" Terry shrugs. "They didn't tell anyone."

"I want to see it."

Terry shakes his head.

"Please …."

He groans but rolls and slides up the bottom of his shirt every so slightly. Thatcher whistles.

"And they're okay with you being—"

"Yeah. We don't talk about it much."

"So who *do* you talk with?"

Terry rolls onto his back. He thinks of Goshen complaining about therapy, all the talk-talk. "Do you make your shirts?" he asks.

"Change of topic—okay. Do you like them?"

"Kinda. Yeah."

"I only started around the time I came out. I needed a statement. The first shirt looked awful. I only had a black Sharpie, and wrote *Riding Time* across the front. And there were plenty of kids who looked at it and squinted and just didn't get it." Thatcher slapped Terry's thigh. "Now I have a drawerful. And better phrases. I keep hoping they'll raise some hackles. But this is a blue state and the worst that happens is a lingering stare, which if they want to do, I'll oblige them."

He catches sight of Terry shaking his head. "Trust me, the swoll hets will start flirting with me before the end of camp."

Terry frowns. "I call bullshit."

"But they do! Their testosterone-soaked brains actually crave attention, and they want to know if the gay kid thinks they're hot. Last year some of the boys began stripping off their shirts right as I was walking by, hoping to make me do a turn-around. And a couple times they'd come up to me in the weight room and flash their abs, asking me if they needed to do more dead bug reps."

"And nothing happened, right?"

Thatcher shrugs but the corners of his lips say otherwise. Terry's stomach lurches off-center. He doesn't want to hear such things, not when it's unfair, unwarranted for Thatcher to hook up with such guys.

"It's never worth it. My father always says, 'Don't shit where you eat.' And I like helping out here. But during the school year …."

"Wait, you go to school here? You're rich?"

"No." Thatcher seems bemused. "My dad moved us here from south Jersey to teach. He pays a fraction of what other parents do."

"No rich boyfriend?" Terry means it sarcastically, but Thatcher doesn't seem bothered.

"The problem with Academy boys is they're thinking matriculation not titillation. Especially the one-percenters, who never get serious. Why bother with a high-school sweetheart when the plan is an Ivy League, and the trust fund is a few years off."

"I think about college. I want go someplace far from Ohio."

"So no one will know the real you?"

"They will. I just can't be the real me now."

"There's no one you want to date back in …?"

"Archbold." Terry thinks for a moment. The only out kid at school is Mateo, who giggles a lot, wears pastel bowties, and is surrounded by a protective orbit of other theater kids. "It's not safe."

"Maybe. But it's got to be lonely."

Terry rolls to the edge of the bed. "Last year, a couple times a girl would start asking her friend, who was sorta seeing a guy on the team. She wanted her to ask him, to ask me if I was interested. It was like a math equation that's impossible to answer right. And they want you at the board trying as everyone watches. I told 'em I was too busy with training, too much homework. But now, with cuffing season ahead, it's going to get sucktacular. I can't be the only guy on varsity without a girlfriend. That'll look—"

"Like you want dick?" Thatcher stretches his arm, his fingers entwined, cracking knuckles. "Don't act all surprised the girls are sweating you."

Terry groans.

"Own your hotness," Thatcher says.

"You think I'm hot?"

Thatcher becomes fascinated with the open pizza box.

Terry's pulse rises anew. "You do!"

"No, I think you're slanky. Eat a slice."

"Not after you slobbered over the pizza."

"Slobbered?" Thatcher takes a slice and puts it in the palm of his hand, holding it aloft.

Terry realizes he's approaching the bed with it, and starts to scurry, but he's too late, as Thatcher throws himself onto the mattress, one hip and elbow pinning Terry to the sheets. The hand with the pizza hovers near Terry's face, even as he struggles pathetically, worse than his first bout against Thatcher, because Terry's low on gas and there's laughter bubbling up his throat. He can only clamp a hand over his mouth to stop both the sound and prevent Thatcher from shoving the slice into his face.

Thatcher gets closer, enough so that those hanging bangs are a soft curtain brushing Terry's forehead. "I'll trade you. One bite for …" He shifts atop Terry, inviting escape, but the younger boy remains motionless, intent on hearing the offer. Thatcher says in almost a whisper, "Whatever you want."

Terry thinks this has cracked open his skull, and the thoughts are leaking out, and it will be impossible for him to scoop everything back inside to even comprehend what was happening. They stare at one another. Thatcher has hazel eyes.

Terry slides his hand off his lips and parts his jaws a little, then a little more.

Thatcher grins, and moves so he can straddle Terry's waist. He lowers the slice but stops just shy of reaching Terry's mouth. Terry has to lift his head from the mattress to take a bite. He chews, slowly, the congealed cheese, and they're still watching each other, almost cautiously. Terry thinks one bite isn't abandoning all reason, but a second … after he swallows, he shows his mouth is empty, ready for another bite. And Thatcher proceeds to feed him until there's only the crust left.

"You're my good boy." Thatcher sits back, still atop Terry. He puts the strip of crust into the corner of his own mouth and wipes his hand clean on his shirt.

"You're a pig."

The older boy's chest becomes a bellows, puffing wide, projecting the remnant of crust almost across the room. "Maybe." Thatcher grabs the bottom of his shirt and peels it up and over his head, revealing a torso with ideal lines, textbook. Terry's eyes begin to roam, to explore, and they promise the rest of Terry's senses that something is going to happen.

"Now, I'm cleaner." Thatcher makes a half-hearted attempt to flatten his hair. "But, you still have to tell me what you want." Fingers start to stroke Terry through his clothes. "Do you need a good friend. Or a great fuck?"

THATCHER MURMURS INTO THE PILLOW, "I need to go."

Terry's hand drifts to the fine hairs covering Thatcher's ass cheeks that are matted with sweat. "Okay," Terry says, because he is sure that he should say something.

"Tomorrow's Game Day." Thatcher finds his phone, and his handsome face is momentarily the bluish center of all creation as he checks the time. "We can hang out afterwards."

From the bed, Terry watches the figure of Thatcher move about the room, searching for his clothes.

"Shit."

"What's wrong?"

"I can't find my t-shirt," Thatcher says.

"Turn on the light."

"No. I'll get it another time."

Terry wonders if he should try and kiss Thatcher goodbye, but the gesture seems both awfully trite after what they've done, and portentous. Instead he offers a monosyllabic word so unremarkable that he forgets whether he said, "Thanks" or "Yeah."

When he's alone, Terry kicks off the bedsheet, because it's damp and cold in spots where things spilled. A tremendous whisper is building at the back of his head, though he's not sure if it's a secret or not. He suspects the whisper is a warning, though.

Despite the late hour he texts his brother: *Do you ever have regrets? I mean after sex.*

He's surprised by the quick response until he remembers it's a Saturday night, and likely Zeke is still awake and about.

Sometimes. I remain the optimist and next time will be better. Why???

Terry appreciates the answer before the question.

Tell you later, is all he can manage.

IN THE MORNING, TERRY SPOTS Thatcher's shirt wedged between the mattress and the wall. He holds it up and counts the stains. The fabric is worn down until it's flimsy and coarse. He crumples it against his face and breathes deep.

He could be a bloodhound, he muses, as he dresses for his early-morning run. But then he chides himself for wanting to run to Thatcher. He tucks the shirt beneath his pillow.

On his second loop around the grounds, he sees the Better Boy that slugged Goshen. The kid's dressed only in rumpled white briefs and wandering about outside the dining hall. On the next pass, Terry spots the kid squatting in the middle of the road that cuts through campus.

Terry swallows his distaste for the kid and turns around. It's a quiet stretch of road, with fancy houses on either end, but eventually there will be traffic.

The kid is staring down at a dead squirrel on the asphalt, and starts to poke it.

"Get away from that," Terry shouts as he comes closer.

The boy looks over his shoulder, and Terry sees his mouth is slack and eyes narrowed. Flies dance across and above it, and some are daring enough to land on the kid's head and arms, but he doesn't bother shooing them off.

Terry's sure he plans on using the carcass as a nasty prank for Goshen. "Go back to bed."

"I'm hungry." The intonation is pure toddler, all exasperation and need.

Terry repeats himself, and the boy remains where he is, but a scowl has been scooped out of his face. "It's your fault I'm hungry! You give blowjobs to cats."

The insult is so ridiculous, so middle school that it surprises rather than stings.

And then the boy pries apart a piece of the carcass and shoves it into his mouth. When he starts chewing with his mouth open, a bit of tongue slips out to wipe at his cracked lips.

Terry stumbles back. He can feel his own throat constricting.

GAME DAY TRANSFORMS THE VAST lower fields of the Academy. A half-dozen colorful cornhole sets are antic; bags of dried kernels leap back and forth across the painted boards like fat fleas. Frisbees in different shades of green make swift yet gentle plays between soccer nets. Terry is briefly distracted by a long line of boys bearing a massive rope for tug-of-war near the football bleachers.

Then a proctor blows the whistle, and Terry has to dodge Abner trying to snatch his tail, a verdant hand towel stuffed into his waistband at his back. His sneakers scuff the vinyl of the worn mat they've dragged outdoors, as he twists, his fingers ever so close to the other boy's tail. A swift jerk and he can hold his prize up high, as those waiting their turn applaud.

His prize is a paper ticket for one of the food trucks parked along a gravel path. Everyone receives them, and so they're worthless.

Abner asks him again about the squirrel as they sip from paper cups filled with crushed ice colored candy-apple red drawn from coolers of sports drink. He's convinced the Better Boys should be locked away. "Little monsters."

Then Terry hears a whistle and turns around to see a pair of proctors carrying mesh bags of equipment. Thatcher wears the Academy sweatshirt, the hood drawn up so his face is almost hidden. But he tips his head, an invitation to follow, and Terry mumbles an excuse to Abner before following Thatcher to to the football field.

The bags are opened and the older boys start throwing out to the campers Velcro belts with either green or white strips.

Millburn is the referee, while Thatcher and the other proctor are team captains. The boys are divided, and Terry feels his insides rumbling as he waits for Thatcher to call out his name, but by the third pick, Terry still hasn't been chosen and there's only two other boys standing beside him. Is this some flirty trick by Thatcher to keep wanting or some cruel dismissal? Terry's relieved when he's picked for the other proctor's team.

The coin's flipped, sides are taken, and when the whistle blows what should have been an eight-person game quickly is distilled to a match between two. Terry gives chase to Thatcher, stepping on his heels, and in turn, Thatcher rushes Terry. The ball is almost ignored.

Terry soon finds the huddle almost hostile. As the proctor cites the play, Piebald spits out the remark he's been chewing. "Why don't you stop chasing your boyfriend, Terry, and play football?"

AFTER THE LOSS, TERRY WAITS for Thatcher to come collect the belt. The older boy looks around a moment, before trapping Terry's hands with the strap.

"There's a river just beyond those trees behind me." His voice drops lower. "We can go skinny-dipping."

"No thanks."

Thatcher's quick smile fades. "Come on. We have almost two hours free before they'll give us something to do."

"*Now* you pick me."

Thatcher tugs on the strap, and Terry digs in with his feet but only for a moment.

The shade from the trees is a relief. Thatcher unzips his hoodie and shows off to Terry the many bruises on his neck above the collar of his t-shirt (*Loves the Butt Drag*).

"Damn," Terry says, realizing the hickeys are his handiwork.

"If anyone sees these ... I need a day or two to come up with something. If anyone found out that we hooked up ... well, you won't be in trouble, but I'll be sunk."

"I didn't know."

They start walking down an obvious trail. Gnats cavort in the air, and try their best to slip into Terry's mouth between breaths.

"Do you regret it?"

Thatcher shakes his head and takes hold of Terry's hand.

Terry's never held another boy's hand, not this way. His palm soon feels hot and sweaty, different from the perspiration earned running around the football field. He feels uncomfortable but he doesn't resist.

At the riverbank Thatcher begins stripping. It's over in seconds, before Terry even conceives of taking off his own shirt. He glances at the pile of clothes Thatcher leaves in the dirt.

"You have to ease into it."

"I have swum outside before. Harrison Lake's not far from—"

"It wasn't pity."

"What?" Terry hesitates dropping his gym shorts even though he's wearing underwear.

"You think last night happened because I felt sorry for you." Thatcher slips under the water for a moment. His shaggy hair doesn't look sexy when wet; it plasters to his skull and makes his head look too large.

"I noticed you on the first day here. I almost ran into you." Thatcher gestures half-heartedly for Terry to join him. "And fuck, did I start sweating you during the lessons."

Still in his briefs and sneakers, Terry sits down on the riverbank. If he enters the river, he'll be bare-skinned and, despite what happened last night, he isn't sure if he wants to hook up with Thatcher again. Especially not if they're going to be honest.

"I think I picked wrong." Terry shook his head. "Maybe I need a friend more than ... this."

He expects Thatcher to try and bullshit him that they are friends, but the older boy begins floating on his back. His chest becomes an island, his limbs reefs, his flaccid dick a topographical curiosity.

"Was it so bad?" Thatcher asks, his face turned to the sky, which July has robbed of clouds.

Terry stares at the ground between his legs. "No." He mumbles to himself how much he liked it, a guilty statement of fact, but the memory is loud in his forebrain.

"It would never have happened in Ohio, right?"

"Right."

Several minutes pass with the only sounds being the occasional splash from Thatcher, the rustle of leaves, and the occasional buzz of a harassing insect.

"I should just be happy ... that this is my summer fling?" Terry asks. "The one that my brother told me I needed?"

"Maybe he was right." Thatcher abandons his mellow sprawl atop the water and starts wading again. "The condoms came in handy."

The laugh dies in Terry's mouth. "So just another Saturday night at the Academy, another hookup."

"It wasn't. I like you. And if anyone found out we fucked, I would lose this gig. And that rep would haunt me in September." Thatcher retreated father from the riverbank. "The only boy who's called a slut is the gay boy."

Terry kicks off his sneakers. "It's easy for you."

"No, it's not." He shakes his head like a wet dog, and in that moment, Terry himself shivers because it's such a sexy move.

He stands up, let's his briefs fall to the ground. "You're such a liar."

The river greets him with a chilly embrace.

"I don't like it much here." Thatcher sighs, as if he needs more oxygen.

"I don't realize how lonely I am unless it's quiet, and so it feels like I'm rushing around, doing everything and anything, all so I don't slow down. And I can't tell my dad how bad it gets some days ... I know he'd say I was squandering my future just to feel happier now."

Terry's eyes are wet. River water? Why was everyone's *now* so terrible?

Thatcher swims closer until they could touch one another. "You leave on Tuesday?" Terry nods. "How many miles is it to Archbold?" Thatcher slips his arms around Terry's submerged chest.

"Hundreds and hundreds."

"Do you need a fuck ... or a good friend?"

The current moves Thatcher's body against Terry's. They drift together a while, and then Thatcher sighs. "We should be getting back to camp."

As he's dressing, Terry says, "I could top you. Tomorrow. At practice."

Thatcher starts to juggle their sneakers. "Gain that weight, and you could pin me."

A SLEEPY TERRY ANSWERS THE repeated knocking at his door expecting it to be Thatcher, but finding Abner standing in the hallway looking disheveled, more than usual, and grinning.

"Get your ass downstairs," he says in a loud whisper.

Several wrestlers from the heftier end of the scale are lounging about Abner's room, watching matches on phones and a tablet, passing water bottles back and forth. Abner takes one from Piebald and presses it against Terry's chest. "This ain't Dasani."

Terry sniffs the top and is rewarded when the volatile fumes rush his nose. He takes a swig, and when the vodka clears his throat clears, asks, "How?"

Piebald slaps Terry's back. He likely doesn't realize how ironic his Bulkeley High Bulldogs shirt is. "I paid a pizza delivery guy a Benny to bring this."

"Piebald's rich?"

They all nod.

Terry realizes he knows so little about most of these guys, despite spending every day amongst them. Does everyone have a secret?

"I love the rich kids," says a wrestler whose face is a pastel pink from sunburn.

"Damn straight," calls out Abner.

Terry knows a shot of vodka has 87 calories. He tries to do the math of how much he has to drink to gain a pound but he loses count as the liquid burns its way down.

"I wish we had cigars," Piebald says.

The tucker sprawled across the floor scowls and shows braces across his teeth. "That would make me puke."

Abner tells him, "No, this will make you puke," as he pours a little of the vodka onto the guy's head.

"Don't waste it," shouts Piebald, reaching for the bottle, and they push him back and shush him.

Abner soon steps close enough for Terry to see that his eyes are shiny like polished glass. "I'm ... it's not true what I told you."

Terry wonders how much he has to drink to achieve that same stare. "What's not?" All he can think of is huckleberries, and if the lie is about their sweetness.

"Millburn. He doesn't have the pull. None of us is getting into here." He spreads his arm wide enough to encompass the entire building. The grounds, too.

"I never believed you," Terry tells him, though, of course, he did.

TERRY STUMBLES NOT BACK TO his room but down the hall to Goshen's door, because Terry has something to tell him—or ask him—though the words are forgotten as he reaches for the door handle. It's unlocked. None of the dorm rooms lock. Don't the rich kids crave privacy? Or are they brazen because of their parents' money?

Goshen is asleep in bed, so Terry hushes himself as he sits down on the floor. His hip nudges the trash bin turned on its side beside the bed, cold hamburger patties piled on a plate atop the base and now teetering. He reaches out, his fingers pushing the plate more than steadying it, and everything topples to the floor.

"Sorry, sorry," he says and stretches out his legs. "That's not going to taste good." He regrets there not being enough vodka left to bring with him. "I guess you stopped eating. I-I didn't see you in the dining hall."

Goshen makes a sound that's not quite a snore. More guttural. And wet.

Terry reaches under his shirt to finger his scar. "I wonder if I have someone inside me, too. But maybe mine's not so bad." He looks over his shoulder at Goshen. "Do they all have to be bad? Suppose what's inside me is the better boy?"

Goshen lets loose another deep snore.

Terry tries to stand but the room begins to spin, so he shuts his eyes and leans his head back to rest against the edge of the mattress.

He's almost asleep when something starts tickling his scalp. Why would the kid be running his fingers through Terry's hair? Terry lifts his arm to get Goshen to stop, but Terry is so tired, and the arm won't move high enough but rather falls back into his lap. He sighs and decides it's not worth the fuss to stop Goshen from stroking his forehead. If only the kid's hand didn't feel so damp, that it might leave a trail as it moves across his skin.

TERRY WAKES IN THE DARK. With a clumsy forearm, he wipes the drool from his lips though the sleeve sticks a little to his face. He scuttles to his feet, and hears a cracking sound. He stares down at the pale and broken moon beneath his right foot. Several moments pass before he realizes it's the plate. Empty.

He turns around and sees the bed is also empty, and the door is wide open. The hall feels deserted, and he checks the time on his phone. It's almost midnight. And he has three messages from Thatcher.

Sry fell asleep he types.

Somethings happening in the commons.

What?

Omw to you

Terry goes into the bathroom to splash his face with cold water. And to see how bad he looks. An askew patch of his hair is stiff to the touch.

Thatcher is waiting for him outside and holds a finger to his lips. "Listen," he whispers.

But Terry doesn't hear anything. Campus is quiet enough that he can hear the trees rustle with the breeze. And he is about to accuse Thatcher of playing a joke, all so they could hook up one more time, when another someone else whispering catches his attention.

Will you ...

Thatcher puts a hand on Terry's shoulder. "I think it's this way." The Academy's lower level can be reached on a paved path that slopes down from the end of the road.

Will you, won't you

"What's going on?"

"I don't know."

Will you, won't you, will you

Terry stops in the middle of the trail down. "Do you see them?"

There's a thin slice of moon overhead, the last in the pie-tin. The figures below are traipsing across the ghostly lines of the soccer field, and start to whirl about one another.

"Are they kids?"

Terry nods.

Will you, won't you, will you, won't you

As Terry and Thatcher reach the field, they see the dancing figures were once Better Boys. Once, because their bodies are slack, heads flopping loose on the necks, legs and arms limp, as if their skeletons were stolen, hijacked to help the stalks rising out of their jaws, stretched inhumanely wide. The glistening, mauve tendrils reflect the moonlight, and their weak glow illuminates the slow dance. Filaments from the thickest stalk's bulbous head extend down to the boy's wrists and shins, moving them like a marionette on its strings.

Thatcher's gasping a litany of swears. Terry's reminded of the rare hothouse orchids at the Toledo Botanical Garden. "Look at them," he says, as Thatcher pulls him back. *They're almost beautiful.*

Will you, won't you, will you, won't you, won't you join the dance?

The Unwelcome Boys start waving their stalks toward the both of them. The nearest lift their host's legs, a bow-legged shuffle, to come closer. Terry reaches out to it, and a tendril, long and supple wraps around his hand, a slick, warm festoon between tucker and that which had been tucked away.

Together they begin to circle one another, the groomed grass cool beneath Terry's feet. He feels the touch of other Unwelcomes as he twirls nearer to, and when the first releases hold of him, another takes his hand. So he finds himself passed back and forth, around and around, glimpses Thatcher calling out to him, screaming his name. And when he reaches the heart of the cotillion, he is grasped by the Unwelcome still wearing Goshen.

A ringlet unfurls from around a bulb and slips beneath the hem of Terry's sweatshirt to tickle as it begins admiring his chest and burnishing the raised tissue of his scar.

Will you won't you

Suddenly Thatcher is by his side and trying to yank Terry loose of the Unwelcome Boy, which quivers as he pulls and there's a wet sound as more of its stalk emerges from Goshen's throat.

Terry hears a snapping sound. The dancers are whipping their uppermost tendrils high in the air and then bowing low toward them both. Terry looks back at the lead Unwelcome, who, with Thatcher's inadvertent assistance, has nearly sloughed off its host.

They're applauding, Terry thinks before he grabs hold of Goshen, thrusting his head down to the ground, then grabbing his legs, an echo of the first maneuver Terry practiced at camp. The husk of the boy collapses beneath Terry with a final whimper of *you won't.*

Free of its burdensome host, the Unwelcome embraces Terry with all its sprigs and shoots, then startles Thatcher when it wraps around him for an instant. As it leaps away, to bound across the field, toward the distant tree line, toward the river. Thatcher is trying to perform CPR on still Goshen.

Terry hears the other Unwelcome convene, eager to be set free. He puts a steady arm on Thatcher's shoulder and tells him, "They need a good friend, too."

WRESTLING CAMP IS OVER. ONCE the collapsed bodies of the Better Boys are discovered on the field, the Academy shuts down all its summer programs, and attendees are told to remain in their dorms while the police come to ask an afternoon of questions. Frightened parents demand answers from the Academy.

Terry's brother calls from a turnpike stop as their mother needs to stretch her bad knee. They should arrive sometime after ten in the morning. Zeke sounds so worried that Terry tells him about the condoms.

Thatcher shows up at his door soon before dinner is to be delivered. "My father's downstairs. He wants you to stay with us tonight." It's the first words Thatcher has said to him this day, and the tone of his voice makes it obvious that the invitation is forced.

Thatcher's dad is a bulkier version of his son, though the hair is shorter, the curls less pronounced. He lacks a bounce to his step, though that may be because he eyes both boys as endangered species.

Dinner is rushed and hushed as none of them can maintain chit-chat. Terry notices that Thatcher grows more withdrawn by the hour until he's barely looking at Terry.

As Thatcher's dad unfolds the sofa bed and readies it for their guest, Terry corners Thatcher in the kitchen.

"You don't want me here."

Thatcher turns to open a cabinet, but Terry shuts it.

"What we did last night—"

"I don't *understand* last night," Thatcher whispers, starts to open a cabinet. "Can you tell me we're not responsible?"

"It was pity."

"What?"

"We ... I did it out of pity. And I don't regret helping them. They were miserable. All of them. And we both can understand what that's like."

Thatcher anxiously looks over Terry's shoulder in the direction of the living room. "I think he knows."

"And?"

Thatcher only shakes his head.

The sofa bed has errant springs, and the spare pillow is lumpy, uneven. Terry waits until after midnight before he throws off the borrowed bedsheet. He walks from door to door and listens at each until he hears the faint sounds of music.

Thatcher sits up in bed. He pulls out one of the earbuds and watches Terry shut the door behind him.

In front of the dresser, Terry strips off his clothes, before opening drawers. When he finds what he was looking for, he holds it in his hands and sits down at the foot of the mattress.

He unfurls the t-shirt for Thatcher to read. *Try My Leg Ride*. Terry slips the shirt over his head, his shoulders. Its fabric is so soft, so light after all the layers he's worn.

A few seconds later, Thatcher moves over and pats the bed, making it clear Terry's welcome.

THE HAFERBRÄUTIGAM

PLÜSCHOW'S LIBIDO DIMINISHED AS HE traveled into Switzerland and finally stepped foot onto German soil. He did not linger on the visage of any of the young men aboard the train cars or waste his imagination on a fleeting glimpse through the window working the fields or travelling the roads. They all wore far too many clothes covering pale skin and he thought of them like snails, a supposed-delicacy only the French could conceive of, poor things that needed the Mediterranean sun, which would divest them of wool and bronze them into something worthy of the palate. By the time he saw the Baltic Sea he suspected he'd have the arousal of an old wether.

His last tryst had been before he had been jailed—had been the *reason* he had been jailed in Rome. It had not even been a particularly satisfying refreshment, yet, his statement to the judge that had he known that the boy lacked promise he would never have taken him to bed did little to mitigate his sentence.

Now he stood at the Konstanz rail station, almost three decades since he had expatriated. His memories of crossing borders so long ago were dim and fragmentary but the station had prospered since then. Italy wanted to retain its rural aesthetic for tourism while Germany had little interest in its past. A nation that stubbornly looked forward. Plüschow would benefit from this by purchasing the latest Voigtländer camera. He brought along his old Century no. 10, small enough for the limited space allowed in a single steamer trunk and not valuable if lost.

He tipped the porter loading his trunk into the cars of the train heading north. One Pfennig, since the man was almost Plüschow's age. He reached for his pocket watch to check the time, felt nothing in his vest pocket and remembered—yet again—he had pawned it to help pay for the trip. He decided against purchasing a beer; it would only be a waste of money as years in Italy had stolen any appreciation he once possessed. As the station clock showed he still had a while before departure, Plüschow wandered and browsed, two acts that did not require expense, not even on an October morning that had some bite in the wind.

When he happened upon a disheveled young man fixated on the resting metal behemoth engine, Plüschow began staring at the youth. He saw nothing socially unacceptable about staring—it was a most efficient and potent means for conveying a host of emotions, especially Plüschow's two favorite: desire and envy, both sides of a single coin, beaten from a golden sliver of Eris's apple.

His assessment of the uncapped young man was that he must be poor, because his clothing looked patched, had what looked like a grain stalk poking out of a worn sleeve and collar, traveling alone, because for the brief time Plüschow stared none had approached him or even acknowledged his existence with a nod or greeting, and he was very handsome, despite the blond hair that needed trimming, with cheeks and chin without a wisp of hair, as Plüschow preferred.

Plüschow casually strode around the young man and noted the fearful expression on the boy's features. He must never have seen a locomotive before and was utterly intimidated by its presence at rest. Once it screeched steam, the young man would likely run back to whatever fields he had just harvested.

Plüschow felt so moved by the sight of such rustic innocence that he was inclined to approach the young man and allay his fears—and Plüschow became aware that this kindness was, in fact, motivated not out of philanthropy but rather a renewed stirring of his cock. He decided then that he owed this boy a debt, one he intended to pay, for returning desire to its proper housing.

So he walked up next to him and said, "I agree they're ghastly, belching terrible smoke, reeking of coal. And the sounds they make. Squeals and roars. Like the engineers are shoving an entire menagerie of animals into the fire. But I wouldn't be too afraid. It is far better than traveling on one's two feet."

No response, not even a glance in his direction. The poor boy must be deaf! Plüschow became more tumescent—a crippled lad was likely never shown affection—and brazen. He repeated a fair amount of what he thought was clever while tugging the boy's sleeve. *That* elicited a reaction, one of genuine shock at being touched. A smell of fresh cut grain came on the breeze.

"You see me?"

"Of course." Plüschow didn't think the question odd, not until much later, on the way to Wismar. "You happen to be standing next to one of the foremost photographers in the world. My eye notices the finer features of young men." He huffed. "Oh, and women. Now tell me, has anyone ever taken a portrait of you?"

The young man blinked and seemed not so much lost in thought but abandoned to it; perhaps Plüschow had happened upon the idiot of Konstanz. But then a smirk transformed the youth's features from merely pleasing to remarkable. "You can see me." He followed this with a chuckle. "And no, I've never met a photographer." His naïve tongue mangled the word.

Plüschow gestured towards the train's passenger cars. "Are you traveling north?"

"I've not made up my mind."

"But you must. If at least to visit Berlin. You'll need a ticket. Forgive me for saying this, but you look rather down on your luck."

The young man leaned in and sniffed by Plüschow's ear. The sudden intimacy made Plüschow coo like a pet dove. He would have gladly handed over his last mark to undress the boy.

"You don't smell like the other men here."

"Be assured that there are no other men like me here. But the scent is from my pomade, purchased in Rome. Olive oil is a marvelous base."

"What's an olive?"

Plüschow slid his arm around the boy and oriented them toward the passenger cars. They began walking together. "A miraculous fruit found in the Mediterranean. The locals press it for oil and the oil is used in everything from cooking to remedies to ... well, lubrication when dry skin would be a terrible bother." Plüschow grinned. "I could purchase a ticket for you ...."

"I am curious ...."

"Never stifle curiosity. Be open to every experience is my belief. No, my religion. You aren't religious?"

The cornsilk-haired youth laughed. "My beliefs are older than you."

"Then I feel young again in your company." Plüschow gestured that they walk up the few stairs to the first-class car where he was berthed—an indulgence bought to calm his anxiety caused by the return home, but most opportune to entertaining company. "Shall we?" He smoothed out his mustache. "You may call me Plüschow." He sat down and patted the space beside him but the youth took the cushioned bench across from him.

"I'm the Haferbräutigam."

"Is that an honorary title or a nickname?"

The young man stretched and put his bare feet on the very spot Plüschow patted. Plüschow scowled, not really annoyed by the dirt visible on the boy's soles—he had wiped away all manner of dust, grime, and even ash from skin, in effect polishing lovers—but rather disappointed he had not taken notice the boy lacked shoes. Plüschow claimed to being discerning and missing such an obvious trait hurt his pride.

"Where are we going?"

"Northwest to Offenburg. My destination is Wismar. Have you heard of it?"

The Haferbräutigam shook his head.

"I was born there," Plüschow said. "The mattress beneath my mother suffered through seven children. I was the first, hopefully anticipated with great enthusiasm. My siblings, well, stain after stain is how I sometimes regard them."

"I was born in a field."

"I would imagine a scene of much ... consternation." Ahh, rustics. They rut in fields, they toil in fields, give birth and die in the fields, or at least, that was the image that came to mind. "I've outlived Bismark, who was born only a few days before me," Plüschow said. "And yet I am not spoken of as often as him. Not very fair, do you think?"

The Haferbräutigam did not comment but gazed out the window as the train began moving.

Plüschow had met a German who had no opinion of Bismark. Remarkable.

The ticket agent arrived. Plüschow handed over his ticket. He was about to search for the funds to pay for the young man's passage when the Haferbräutigam smiled at the uniformed man, who tipped his cap and then left without saying another word.

"I am not the only one to notice your charms."

"So, funeral, wedding, or to make amends?"

"Pardon?"

"You smell foreign, sound foreign, so you have been away a long time. You are travelling back to the cradle but spending money to do so. Men return from a long absence for a funeral, a wedding, or—"

Plüschow held up a hand. "I dislike funerals and weddings. For different reasons, mind you. And I never apologize."

"So then?"

"A family reunion." Plüschow left unsaid the difficulty in accepting the invitation. He did not recognize the name—apparently a grand nephew; he had no idea how many children his siblings had engendered, and their offspring's offspring ... and so forth. He took out his pipe and tobacco while the Haferbräutigam watched him and flinched when Plüschow lit the match.

"So, my little alienist," Plüschow encouraged the tobacco to burn, "I shall admit to being a scoundrel."

The Haferbräutigam grinned. "Thank you for warning me."

With the pipe stem clenched between his teeth, Plüschow turned toward the Haferbräutigam's bare feet. No stockings and so the skin above the ankles waited to be stroked. Plüschow risked resting a palm over the round bone above one foot.

"I have been in prison," he said.

"Are you dangerous?"

Plüschow shrugged. "Are you frightened?"

"No. No man has ever frightened me."

Plüschow squeezed the ankle. He expected hard bone but the foot gave a little and he heard a crackling sound. Perhaps the child was ill?

"So you are a felon?"

"I am. Dare you guess my crime?"

"Is this a game?" asked the Haferbräutigam.

"It can be."

"What are the rules?"

"Are you hungry?"

"Always. I never get full."

"Ahh, the appetites of the young. Older men have more discriminating appetites. Three guesses to my crime. If your deductions are correct, I shall treat you to a sumptuous meal of your choice in the Bistrowagen."

"And if I always guess wrong?"

Plüschow slid his hand an inch higher up the Haferbräutigam's shin. "I satisfy my tastes here."

"Agreed."

"Marvelous," Plüschow said. "Before we begin, to be fair, I will allow you to ask one simple question of me—which I swear to respond with the utmost honesty—before each guess."

"You're being too kind."

"Am I? I suppose a face like yours causes me to let down my guard." Plüschow examined the Haferbräutigam's toothy smile. He realized that he may have been too kind, indeed. "Oh, but you cannot, of course, ask me why I went to prison ... that would be rather a cheat. The questions have to do with—"

"With appetites," the Haferbräutigam said. "So tell me, do you prefer honey or sugar?"

"Such an odd question to begin with. The answer is sugar."

"You were jailed as a thief."

"While I have been accused of taking innocence on occasion, that was not my crime," Plüschow said.

"Do you prefer capon or hen?"

"Ahh, I suppose you know the answer before asking." He slid his hand further. The skin beneath his fingers was dry, so very dry. "Capon."

"You were jailed as an agitator."

"I definitely live an unrepentant life at odds with the sanctimonious mores of those in charge around me, but I roused no rabble."

"Do you eat the seed of the fruit?"

When Plüschow said "Yes," he felt a decade younger and smothered by the layers of clothing he wore.

"You were caught fucking a boy born in springtime."

Plüschow cursed as his thumb tamped down on the bowl of his pipe and singed the pad of skin.

The Haferbräutigam laughed and, in a most nimble move, took seconds to stand and jump over Plüschow's knees.

"Well done." Plüschow cleared his throat. He felt rather distressed as much as disappointed as a vague sense of being cheated nagged him. "Though before your last query, I found myself distracted with the thought of the Bistrowagen's menu, and I am rather relieved your guess was so lucky."

Plüschow lead the way through the train cars and to the crowded Bistrowagen, so crowded there was not a single empty table. The smell of fresh coffee and grilled meat mingled in the air. Plüschow had not dined on any traditional German dish since his youth. Recognizing dishes was akin to paging through photographs, seeing faces, and remembering the taste of the models who'd once posed for him. A pinched-faced woman dressed in a widow's wedding dress cut across cervelat while her equally dour companion, a man with white tufted eyebrows that made the top half of his bald head appear alert while his drooping mustache lulled the remainder, sampled Lard d'Arnad and black bread.

"I should have said 'honey,'" Plüschow muttered to himself. His stomach felt empty, ignored. "Speck needs honey." He leaned down to the old man and recommended he ask the server for some. The man ignored the suggestion, most rudely without even a "Thank you" or nod.

The Haferbräutigam went to the next table. He took the fork from a businessman's hand without resistance and dropped it onto the wood table. At the moment it clattered, the man left his seat, abandoning both plate full of food and table. The Haferbräutigam then gestured for Plüschow to sit with him at the table. He swept the plates to the floor. Not a single head turned at the crashing of dishes and glassware.

"I don't want you watching me eat."

"Something very wrong is happening," Plüschow said. A server carrying a platter stepped onto a broken plate without concern and moved right past them. "Pardon me ..." But no one would pay attention to Plüschow, whose stomach growled.

The Haferbräutigam smirked. "I want to thank you for the game earlier. The last time … I think was a young mother. There were no locomotives back then. Carriages with real horses. Don't be sad, she lost too. But I do love to play. You never had a chance of winning, and I could never have sated what you craved. So you have to go hungry now."

The Haferbräutigam sniffed the air. Plüschow's old nose did the same and noted that all the various odors of food had vanished from the Bistrowagen. It smelled like a barn instead.

Plüschow sneezed, which elicited giggles from a nearby table. Not from the father or mother but the two young girls across from them. They wore fine dresses and shiny shoes. Light blue ribbons decorated their plaited dark hair. They stared at Plüschow—no, at the Haferbräutigam—and smiled and giggled more. One whispered in the other's ear.

The Haferbräutigam turned his head with the slow yet fluid motion of an owl following the sound of a mouse among the leaves. When he smiled at the girls, his chin grew another two inches to accommodate a jaw with so many teeth, and the scent of grain became cloying.

"What are you?"

"Not so different from you." The Haferbräutigam did not look away from the animated girls, whose titters and whispers to each other now consummated with them waving hello and blowing him kisses. He gestured for them to come close and they nearly tumbled off the bench in their enthusiasm to approach.

Plüschow shook his head. "I refuse to believe we're alike in any manner."

The Haferbräutigam reached out and petted more than stroked each girl's long hair, their shoulders and small waists. He touched their cheeks. His smile never waned. A long strand of glistening saliva dropped from the side of his mouth closest to Plüschow.

"I don't want you watching me eat," the Haferbräutigam said again.

The girls took hold of his hand and tugged him to his feet as if it were a game—he was not much taller than either and yet, he *loomed* over them once on his feet. The girls' giggles scraped along Plüschow spine.

"I won't …" He lost whatever threat he had sought to voice when the Haferbräutigam looked at him. *The wolf from fairy tales stands before me. He has hens in his mouth and dares the old rooster to raise a cry.*

"Remember, these are my prize for winning the game, Herr Plüschow. Remain humble in defeat and I may one day return the generosity, but," the Haferbräutigam lifted both arms, like a hunter raising the brace of hares he had caught to show off his good fortune—and the girls kept giggling even though their faces contorted in the pain of having their small arms wrested high almost out of the socket, "if you cry foul, then you will regret ever leaving that prison."

Plüschow made a show of covering his mouth while rubbing his mustache back and forth. He felt sick, as if he had witnessed an act of pure cruelty. Yet he did not doubt the threat made by the terrible spirit he had invited aboard the train. Yes, that was the worst: who was to blame for the abduction, the fate of those girls on than him?

As soon as the Haferbräutigam and his merry prizes had left the Bistrowagen, Plüschow sat down on the vacated bench opposite the girls' parents.

"Quickly! While I cannot myself rescue your daughters, there might still be time for you!" They glanced up at him from their plates, their forks, their knives. "At the very least demand the conductor stop the train before …" He could not bring himself to say what the Haferbräutigam's intentions were because not only did it sound insane—a dashing man with a wolf's teeth tearing apart little girls? The stuff of fairy tales, indeed!—but he did not want to terrify the parents. Nothing in nature sounded worse than a hysterical woman's cries except the banal promises by the husband with the Sisyphean task of comforting her.

"We are so proud of our Häschen." A forkful of sauerkraut followed the wife's words. She had damp lips and dry eyes.

"And to think I didn't have to spend a pfennig on a dowry. Oh, these are tough times, tough times." The husband chewed a piece of kassler openly. He was missing several teeth, which meant he favored one side of his mouth.

Plüschow gripped the edges of the table. He could not understand their unruffled demeanor. He wanted to add their plates to the mess on the train car's floorboards. "Don't you care that they were taken?"

"We must remember to come back in the spring," the wife said to her husband.

Plüschow stood. He cuffed the husband's hat off his head. The fellow scowled. "Do you even remember their names?"

Plüschow did not want to know the answer and headed back to the passenger cars.

He collapsed on the seat beside the window and drew the shade down.

He stared at his hands, both of them, first at the palms. He thought about the rustics of Italy he dealt with so often that he could guess correctly the course of their day from waking to sleep. What they ate this season and when. What they worried about—nearly always money, which was why so many of them agreed to let Plüschow photograph their children for centesimi, lira if he brought them back to his studio in Naples or Rome. He knew which fathers and mothers suspected he wanted to fuck their sons. He knew which fathers and mothers sold them their sons.

But this? The Haferbräutigam?

Plüschow never left a boy with so much as a scratch.

Those girls would be scratched. He remembered the dry flesh of the Haferbräutigam. His teeth ....

The simple folk around Naples believed in *folletti*, spirits, goblins. They blamed many things for bad crops, poor health, lost animals, lost children, lost loves. Rather than look around them and see that the twentieth century had arrived, rather than welcome it, they sought refuge in the ignorance of the past. And not simply the lingering, whimpering final years of the last century but rather their beliefs were consistent with a man from 1805, say. An Italian farmer could spend an entire month in the company of such a superannuated figure and never see the difference between one and the other. But not the German people—they understood the momentum of progress, on the land and on its people.

Or so Plüschow always believed. He could never have run his studio in, say, Württemberg. His dwindling patrons did not want nude boys in German meadows. Or dirty lads working in factories.

Or photographs of girls. No, not girls in pretty dresses with blue ribbons. Not ripped girls.

He needed a drink. He felt dry, parched, his hands rubbing together sounded unpleasant. Those girls would be scratched. The Haferbräutigam's teeth ....

No, he should not blame himself. The parents were right there, the Bistrowagen full! He had no notion of that ... thing's true nature. Or its appetite. He was lucky to have survived the encounter. Should he feel guilty because his heart still beat? He suffered. His heart felt erratic in his chest as if the organ itself knew fear. He doubted he would forget this day. Why should the girls' parents ... and the others present ... all masticating like sheep ... why should he alone remember?

Perhaps his mind was too keen to be taken in by sorcery? Should a man of this new era look askance? No. He must look forward even if some tears were shed.

But a bottle of something strong would not be refused by anyone sane. He lifted up the shade and watched the landscape roll towards him, moved his head and saw what fell away. He would be thankful if they pulled into Offenburg Station early.

D IS FOR DELICIOUS

MS. GRACKLE HEARD THE WORD "Scrumptious" whispered in her ear as she tended Chucky Goldberg's skinned knee. But then, all week long she'd been hearing voices.

When she reached into a glass jar for a gauze pad to cover his scrape, she found instead a folded strip of paper covered with rows of colored dots. It would have fallen on the worn linoleum if Chucky hadn't grabbed one trailing end. As he giggled away, she checked the drawer where she kept spare supplies and found it full of pink tufts of cotton candy.

The oversweet smell brought back memories of a distant summer during high school spent behind the counter of the Snack Shack. Memories of Effie Lintz, who had a gap between her front teeth that made the young Miss Grackle stare and tingle all over—a gap meant more for tongues than spit.

Uncomfortable with dredging up the past, she slammed the drawer shut. Chucky, still sweaty from gym class, jumped. The poster of *Inner Workings of the Nose* fell to the floor.

"My mother won't let me eat sugar." Chucky crunched and chomped on the candy. "She wants me *enthusiastic*, not manic, she always says." Chucky had already taken his daily dosage of Ritalin.

By the time Chucky had torn off every dot—leaving his slick tongue swirled with color—Ms. Grackle had found enough tiny bandages to cover

113

his kneecap in a patchwork pattern. "Cool," he said, and dropped the empty paper on the floor before running back to the classrooms.

Ms. Grackle dumped all the candy in the battered trashcan. She sat down at her desk and discovered a chocolate bar in the snout of the piggy bank the fifth graders had bought her as a retirement present. She tugged the bar free.

Candy. For almost a week she had been finding shiny gumballs, cellophane-covered nougats, and black licorice crows littered around her office. Tongue depressors replaced by lollipops fashioned from pink or purple sugar. At first, she had thought it was a prank played by the children or by Mr. Crad, the French teacher, who last year had sent an entire giggling class to her complaining not of cooties but coutés. But the treats now appeared so suddenly that nothing scientific or educational could be behind them.

She washed the milk-chocolate residue from her hands with antibacterial soap. When she turned back, a woman in her thirties with long black hair and an even longer green-apple-shaded dress had taken her chair. The woman looked familiar despite her smile. The icicles hanging from Ms. Grackle's windowsill this past winter had looked less white, less sharp than those teeth.

"You look hungry," the woman said.

Ms. Grackle stepped back. Her stomach *did* grumble. She had packed a tuna-fish-and-tomato sandwich but when lunchtime came the soggy wheat bread and pasty fish had been less than appealing, with a smell worse than any dumpster. Had she missed an expiration date on the can? Mrs. Towfer, the second-grade teacher, had rescued the sandwich at the last moment, as Ms. Grackle brought it near the garbage pail. She had watched as Mrs. Towfer's lips had smacked away while the stink of a dirty aquarium hung about the faculty lunchroom.

She couldn't remember the last time she had eaten *anything*. Last week? She felt a bit hollow. Not weak, but definitely not all there, either, as if with every missed meal a part of her went missing as well.

"If you're my replacement," said Ms. Grackle, looking the woman over, admiring her—when you're a senior citizen, you can do so without seeming lecherous—"then I am sorry to tell you the office won't be vacant until summer school."

The woman laughed with a handsome resonance that lingered a second too long in the air. "I'm not surprised you've forgotten me. A bit hurt,

114

though." She slapped the daily calendar off the desk. "Congratulations for your forty-five years at Marchen Elementary this coming Friday, dear. I'm here to serve as your retirement advisor."

"Did the principal send you? The union?"

"No. I represent a much older, more distinguished group: witches. You're a member whether you like it or not."

Ms. Grackle winced. Now and then, a child might smile at her, but nearly five decades of hearing "Cackle Grackle" sing-songed had left her tender. She often thought children teased the school staff for the same reason a caged canary mocked a cat: resentment for being kept penned for hours for its own good. And didn't the students only associate her with hurt, stinging antiseptic, and nausea?

"I'm sorry, Miss—"

"Hamilton. Remember me yet?" The woman rubbed her hands together. White powder drifted across the speckled linoleum floor. "No? Well, let's take a ride."

"School's not over, Miss Hamilton." Though her official day ended at 2:30 p.m., Ms. Grackle often stayed well past 4:00. She'd drive to the library or walk in the park if the weather was nice. Her small apartment felt rather like a jail cell these days.

"Hamilton. No Miss. Three syllables are enough. And they're not going to fire you for playing hooky this once." She pulled a gold-foil-wrapped coin the size of a quarter from her own ear and dropped it into the piggy bank.

"I'd be setting a bad example for the children, being in the car with a total stranger." Ms. Grackle left unsaid how she didn't trust Hamilton even though she did seem more familiar by the moment.

"I can ask nicer." Hamilton snapped her fingers and a dish of glazed donuts appeared. Ms. Grackle could smell how fresh they were. "Pretty please with sugar on top." Hamilton's smile belonged to a wild animal. "Or we can meet for dinner tonight."

Dinner with such a woman? Ms. Grackle felt her breath hitch in her lungs as if she were asthmatic. Too many years ago she could have refused with the slightest of smiles, the ones martyrs prided themselves on wearing. Now, she shook her head, as if in a daze. Her fingers reached for her car keys. Dinner with such a woman was more dangerous than an accident on the road.

Ms. GRACKLE DROVE A BATTERED two-door hatchback, so rusty that she'd nicknamed it "Ol' Tetanus." Last fall, she had promised herself a brand-new sedan with soft seats and air conditioning as her first retirement extravagance. But the newspaper reviews of automobiles she'd cut out as promising had been ignored for the past few months.

Hamilton guided her through unrecognizable parts of town. And Hamilton's clothes had, well, *changed*, when she wasn't looking. Now, with an almost demure air about her as she sat in the passenger seat, Hamilton wore a starched white nurse's uniform, one she'd last seen in some Shirley Eaton film on Turner Classic Movies.

They parked in front of a long building with a slouching roof and dangling shutters on the windows. The sign out front read "The D'Aulnoy Shelter for Subsistence Beldames." The lawn was brown and dead. A very old woman, winter-twig thin and wearing only a bathrobe and slippers, plodded along the grounds.

"Is this a nursing home?" Ms. Grackle asked.

"Of sorts. Though the witches inside would insist it's more of a health retreat."

"She doesn't look healthy."

"No, not at all." Hamilton left the car. "Come on."

Witches cannot exist, Ms. Grackle told herself. *Such things were never mentioned at Seton Hall.*

The old woman in the bathrobe muttered, "Dry as a bone inside," as they passed her.

As a trained nurse, Ms. Grackle knew that "dry as a bone" was wrong. Large bones had spongy marrow and manufactured blood cells. She thought the air inside the shelter should be compared to something else. Dust maybe. Or brittle newspaper left in the attic for a hundred years. Her skin flaked after a few steps down the hallway. Flour sprinkled down from Hamilton's fingernails like fine ash.

The women living at the shelter each looked older than the next. Tired skeletons covered in ivory skin, tufted at the skull with cotton candy-colored hair. Lemon-drop eyes blinked at Ms. Grackle. She saw the old women— not witches, she told herself—turn away from Hamilton.

"They look starved." To her amazement, she saw Hamilton was crying.

"Yes, it's tragic."

Abuse was common at nursing homes. She often worried what would happen to her when she could no longer care for herself. But the school district was quite clear that retirement at her age was *mandatory*.

"Shouldn't we be calling the police?"

"Do you remember the story of Hansel and Gretel? Witches need to eat children. All that baby fat is so nutritious." Hamilton wiped her face clean of the tear tracks and the bit of drool slipping from her mouth. "But some are too afraid to nibble. So they shrivel."

Ms. Grackle stared at Hamilton. Her face was plump, her skin smooth. "You look ... well fed."

The witch—Ms. Grackle had no doubts now—smacked coral-tinted lips. "I have a thing for Brownies."

An aroma, both domestic in its simplicity and decadent in its promise, of baking chocolate drifted from Hamilton like perfume and revived in Ms. Grackle the memory of their first encounter.

SHE HAD YET TO CHOOSE a major. Her mother had approved Seton Hall's Catholic education as a first step toward vocation—she should become a teaching nun. Miss Grackle was uncertain. One autumn evening that remembered summer's warmth, she left the dorm with a sweater held in her fist. It trailed through fallen leaves behind her. And when she breathed in the night air, the scent of warm brownies filled her.

She *had* to follow the smell, and wandered to the grounds of the nursing school. She found the second-floor window, open and bright, and the tray cooling on the sill. Then came Juliet.

No, her name was not really Juliet. But Miss Grackle had just read Shakespeare's play days before—and had cried over how stupid Juliet had been to waste her life— and the sight of a wistful girl coming to the window, resting her elbows beside the baking pan to sigh into the night, filled the young Miss Grackle to the brim with ache. And maybe, just maybe, she whispered up, "That I might touch that cheek."

The not-Juliet looked down then and smiled and made her feel like the heir to the Montague fortune.

"Stargazing?" Not-Juliet asked.

Miss Grackle nodded and smiled ever-so-small at the joke the girl could not understand.

"I baked brownies." Not-Juliet lifted one side of the pan and the rich smell actually doubled. "I was pricked too often today."

"Pricked?" Miss Grackle felt her face grow warm. Warmer than the pan, she suspected.

Not-Juliet grinned. "Be a good girl." She stretched out an arm. "In class. We take turns giving needles. No matter how you try to make it a game, it hurts."

One of the saints—her mother was always quoting them—had said, "This fire of Purgatory will be more severe than any pain that can be felt, seen or conceived in this world." Miss Grackle had always thought that a bit of hyperbole; wasn't Hell true torture?

But now she understood what the saint meant—nothing seemed so uncomfortable, so restrictive as standing ten feet below such a pretty girl while the air was warm and sweet. She could stand on her toes, lift her arms high, and still not-Juliet would be out of reach. And she wanted nothing more than to brush her fingers against what promised to be the softest cheek in the world.

"I might share." Not-Juliet reached into the pan and pulled loose a hunk of brownie. She held it over Miss Grackle's head. "Would you like that?"

Feeling like a hound eager to please her mistress, Miss Grackle nodded fast. "Ever so much."

Then not-Juliet brought the brownie to her lips and took a bite. Crumbs fell. "Go to the door. I will let you in."

MS. GRACKLE'S LEGS TREMBLED. SHE found a comfy chair. Across from her, another old woman wearing bland pajamas stared at wallpaper decorated with rows of vegetables. A tray across her lap held a plastic bowl of colorless mush and a matching teacup of steaming water that looked sad without a tea bag.

"You finally remember me."

Ms. Grackle nodded. "But you look—"

"You are what you eat. A retirement benefit, if you will." Hamilton reached out but stopped just shy of Ms. Grackle's stiff, gray curls. "After the school bell rings at 2:30 this Friday, you could be like me."

"I ... I ... I want to say 'nonsense.'"

"Time to grow up. We're not born this way. Long ago, spinster aunts became the witches. Now it's school nurses and lunch ladies." Hamilton squatted beside the chair. "Don't you want revenge for years of tears and whining, picking lice and wiping vomit?"

Was that why the school board hadn't bought her a gold watch? Did they know? "If I don't eat children ...."

Hamilton sighed. "I'll have to bring you here. And they'll feed you slop."

Ms. Grackle didn't want to eat children. Besides seeming wrong, it seemed so unpractical. Maybe all the beldames needed were vitamins and more fiber. She plucked at a tattered strip of the wallpaper hanging from the plaster. A piece of a radish tore free.

The smell of boiled vegetables sickened her. "And the candy?"

"Conjured for the children. We can't stomach sweets."

At least she wouldn't get diabetes. Shaken, she rose from the chair. Without another word to Hamilton—she could not even process the thought of her looking so ... so desirable after all these years—she headed back to the shelter's front door. She passed a parchment-skinned woman in a wheelchair reading a coloring book of the alphabet. Cartoon children smiled and danced around gigantic letters. The woman had the pages close to her face. Ms. Grackle heard murmuring and stopped. She brought her ear close to the woman's dry mouth and heard: "D is for delicious."

HER CAR STALLED ON THE drive back home. While she struggled to start the engine, a pack of kids on rollerblades chased one another on the sidewalk. Ms. Grackle frowned at their lack of helmets. She watched as one boy hit a crack and toppled onto the pavement. She winced, but the boy picked himself up, wiped the grit from scraped palms, and followed the others.

If I had fallen, she thought, *I'd have broken my wrists. Maybe a hip.* Why were only children permitted to play, to waste afternoons and weekends without care?

She tried to have a normal evening at home. Sitting on the sofa, her plate on her lap, she watched a cable show on anorexia surgery while poking the microwave dinner (a deflated burrito) but never taking a bite. One young lady's arms had become excessively hairy, the stressed body's attempt to keep itself warm. Even her eyes held a trapped-in-the-cage wariness. Ms. Grackle wondered how many women became monsters. She pushed the plate from her lap. It slipped and landed on the floor, the plate cracking, the burrito leaking refried, reheated bean paste onto the thinning carpet. As she went on her hands and knees to clean the mess, she was struck with the thought that monsters in those awful movies always chased after women.

Would it finally be socially acceptable for her to do the same?

AT SCHOOL THURSDAY, JOHNNY MEIR came to have a splinter removed. He devoured two snicker doodles from a new tin on her desk before she could stop him. "I can stuff five of these in my mouth," he mumbled around a mouthful. "An' I once ate a hot dog squirted with thirteen packets of mustard. Holly Riggenbach dared me." He reached for another cookie. "So I hadda." Johnny would come into her office twice a week complaining of stomach aches.

Though she had the tweezers in hand, Ms. Grackle used her dentures to remove the sliver of wood in the fleshy part of his finger. A single drop of blood met the tip of her tongue. In all of her life she had never tasted anything so scrumptious, so delicious. As if sunshine had masqueraded as syrup in his veins. She stood there, still tightly holding his hand, leaning so close she could almost breath him in, guilty over what she had done, but tempted to take just another teensy taste, maybe a nibble.

Johnny stared at her, wide-eyed. She dropped his hand. "You bit me," he half-whispered, half-whined, before running off.

Ms. Grackle locked the door to her office. The poster on the back offered a brightly colored pyramid teaching what foods should be eaten. She stabbed at the purple triangle that represented five ounces of meat a day. *Go lean on protein.* Children weren't part of a healthy diet.

DESPITE FEELING HOLLOW, SHE CHOSE to walk home. Early June seemed far too eager to herald summer, and her old car would have been an oven. The dry heat rising from the pavement made her feet ache, though, and reminded her that she was old, that every step forward was a step closer to finality.

Unless she chose to sample children.

Death had kept her from ever acting on her attractions. A stroke felled her father sophomore year, and Miss Grackle had moved back home, where for years, her mother's Catholic shadow reared all three heads. Guilt. Prudence. Shame. She had not been with another girl, let alone woman, since Hamilton.

And when she finally found herself free of parental demands and guilt, she was middle-aged, bogged down by the familiar routine of the school day, fearful that if she ever did come out she'd lose her job. By the time New Jersey offered to shelter her attractions, she was so close to retirement that the idea of coming out seemed ridiculous. And who would want a fossil like her, anyway?

Then, just weeks ago, while watching *Julie & Julia*, Ms. Grackle had felt a stirring in her gut, an almost forgotten sensation of heat and ache that she worried was more loneliness than hunger. She now imagined Hamilton, wearing a gingham dress covered with a spotless apron, and that stirring returned.

At the intersection, a crowd of boys and girls—what was the collective noun, a recess of children?—surrounded an ice cream truck, their hands either clawing at the air or clutching dripping cones and popsicles. She frowned at the display of such quick-and-ready consumption. Certain children deserved a nip or two. That Johnny Meir, or Richie Cowles who faked a nosebleed last month to get out of a quiz. But not every student at Marchen should be fricasseed, especially not the poor, shy girls who boys forced into silence. One did not have to be a gourmand.

Life at the shelter couldn't be any more the lonesome Purgatory than what she'd been living.

The truck's jingle echoed inside her. She wondered if witches were all hollow. The way she felt right now.

AT 2:30 THE FINAL BELL rang. Ms. Grackle's mouth and hands felt raw and hot. Her dentures popped out like novelty teeth. She gnashed new teeth. Aromatic flour drifted down from her fingers. Other scents came to her but mostly she breathed in the stink of children, a thousand times worse than pig or chicken. And she knew the only way to make a grubby boy or disheveled girl less fetid required cooking. Drool spilled from her lips. She was so hungry that the little blonde girl brushing her teeth on one hygiene poster looked appetizing, as if she had a mouthful of whipped cream instead of toothpaste.

"Happy birthday." Hamilton sat on the padded bench. She wore a suit in light pink and white and a matching pillbox hat. Pearls, so large they could have been jawbreakers, were strung around her neck. "I'd bake you a cake, but now you could conjure one yourself by waving your hands."

Grackle thought about the slices of homemade carrot cake with cream-cheese icing that she had stolen bites of as a kid at the Snack Shack. Her fingers itched and then she held a thick slice on a paper plate. But she thought the cake looked as worthless as she felt; what good did all the sweets in the world serve if there wasn't a child enjoying them, growing fat and toothsome?

"Not bad." Hamilton clapped. "So, have you decided on a diet? I don't mean to rush but there's more to magic than creating sweets. There's no sense in training you if you plan on not devouring kids."

Grackle thought back to the old women in the shelter. "And my decision is final?"

"Well, yes. Traditionally—"

"Habits, especially bad habits, are meant to be broken."

"So you'd rather starve?"

Grackle went over to her supply closet and gave it one last good tug open. She looked at all the tubes of ointment and packages of gauze and splints. So many injuries so often caused by reckless children. Maybe she could eat one or two a week, but there'd still be enough to fill the halls with mayhem. Enough to feed a horde of witches. Since last night she'd been plotting.

"Magic makes the gingerbread houses, right?"

Her old friend nodded. "A skilled witch can conjure nearly any object."

"Delicious," Grackle said as she stroked Hamilton's cheek. She cackled and hoped that some child passed close enough to hear the sound and shiver.

"Here's my thought …."

A GLEAMING WHITE ICE CREAM truck that would never need gas or a tune-up arrived outside a neighborhood soccer field. The vanilla icing over panels of graham cracker gleamed like fresh paint. A mob of children surrounded the truck and screamed for treats. Behind the steering wheel, Hamilton hummed a melody and the speakers atop the truck chimed. Grackle, young and lovely in a matching, bone-colored uniform, stepped outside and began handing out free ice cream cones and sandwiches. A trip to the beach yesterday to test their conjured truck had been a delight and provided her first good meal in weeks.

She opened the metal doors at the back of the truck. "There's more sweets inside. Come in, come in, children. Plenty of room." She herded boys and girls inside and threw wide the freezers, which yawned deep and cold and full of the finest frozen treats any child could imagine tasting.

The rear doors sealed. Hamilton stepped on the gas. As Grackle counted children with dripping smiles and sticky hands, she hoped that the shelter's kitchen had roomy ovens, and that the witches who once refused to feed on children had grown hungry enough over the years to change their minds.

THE UNSOLVED "CASE OF THE CLUB TARRARE"

WIGGINS IS A PENNILESS COVENT Garden Tadzio. I want to tell stories about him. I wish I knew his given name. In my imagination, the only parts of him not covered in dirt and soot are his long eyelashes. He shivers beneath patched clothes. He's left-handed and an orphan and he deserves adventures. He is the only one of the Baker Street Irregulars, that gang of barefoot youths Sherlock Holmes used as his eyes and ears throughout wretched London, named by Doyle. Wiggins is a playful name, don't you think?

When I was a child, I adored the Holmes stories. I wanted to be Wiggins, who I believed had a much more extraordinary life than my own.

Wiggins appears only in *A Study in Scarlet* and *The Sign of the Four*— canonical but minor. His voice is described as high; Doyle never allowed Wiggins to reach puberty. His last appearance would have been in September of 1888.

In 1891, Holmes plunged down the Reichenbach Falls and was presumed dead. He hid from the world for four years. He abandoned Watson and the Irregulars. How would an adolescent Wiggins survive living on the streets of London without his benefactor? Some fifteen-year-old boys found themselves working as telegraph messengers. A few working out of a building on Cleveland Street earned several shillings being prostitutes. Even Prince Eddy used the boys. The scandal, when it broke, captivated the nation.

Rereading Doyle, I found a reference in *The Hound of the Baskervilles* to Holmes hiring a telegraph boy to deliver a message via bicycle. I think that if Wiggins knew this—1889, he would have been thirteen, too young to be employed at Cleveland Street but he must have known that older men would pay to fuck boys—he would have been jealous, so very jealous. Of course, maybe Holmes did nothing more than hand the unnamed telegraph boy a piece of paper.

At fifteen, I enjoyed riding my bicycle. I often visited Robbie Ostroff, whose house was close enough that I could walk to it in minutes, but when you're visiting a boy you have a crush on, you feel the need to rush there. You want to arrive out of breath.

Though he was a senior, Robbie must have enjoyed my attention. He wrestled, was stout, with no visible neck. He had a sparse mustache and his forearms and calves were thick and covered in dark hair. Sometimes he wore old t-shirts that he had outgrown and I had difficulty not staring at the forest that sprung between his wide stomach and the upper span of his crotch.

His room reeked of adolescence and sports. I didn't know what to do with half the things he played with. It would not have taken a great detective to realize I was gay but Robbie made Lestrade look astute.

Holmes needed a seven-percent cocaine solution to quiet his boredom and anxieties. Robbie enjoyed quiet interludes, 300mg of methaqualone, stolen from his mother's medicine cabinet.

I find one scene captivating in Tom Ford's otherwise mundane *A Single Man*: a golden-hued youth fresh from the shower seeks to seduce Colin Firth. My imagination replaces Nicholas Hoult with a teenage Wiggins, who has been ordered by Holmes to scrub away the patina of grime. Out of the bath, out of the water closet, steps a hesitant Wiggins, pink-skinned for the first time he can remember, damp-curled, an Irregular made aboveboard and clutching a towel about his waist. He walks to where he sees Holmes reclining on the divan but finds him unresponsive. A lascivious moment becomes languid with disappointment as an empty hypodermic rolls when Wiggins's toes nudge it on the Oriental rug.

Would Wiggins resist temptation? Prince Charming found a beautiful maiden asleep and he only sought to kiss her. Prince Eddy sought more from those in bed. I remember Robbie Ostroff partially undressed, his jeans unzipped and one hand just resting along the elastic band of his stark white briefs, the tips of his ring finger and pinkie actually beneath the cotton and atop the coarse dark pubes.

When had Wiggins first tasted cock—who else wonders when their favorite fictional characters lose their innocence? Would it have been with one of the other Irregulars, a smaller boy, his penis stiff with excitement at one more secretive (and illegal!) act, and would it not have the taste of the street on it, foreskin pushed back, skin coated with an overripe grease that might have made Wiggins gag? I think erotica tells lies about what giving a blowjob is like.

I have never been a Prince Charming.

My untitled Victorian story begins with ruffians—the word alone conjures a sense of time and place and squalor—beating fifteen-year-old Wiggins senseless in an alley. I want the reader to sympathize with Wiggins but do not plan on revealing what he has done to deserve the contusions. I myself do not even know. Maybe he has gambling debts. I am a gambleholic. Perhaps, drunk on gin, he is a braggart. Perhaps while serving as an Irregular he had observed things best left unsaid. And unseen.

Whatever his trespass, Wiggins pays for it dearly with the next sentence: *The steel of the knife left an acrid taste on his tongue, which wriggled like a worm when presented by any beak.* The ruffians cut out his tongue. I wrote of blood filling his mouth and the memory of Robbie Ostroff's penis between my lips, his semen spurting on to my tongue and leaving a taste that was disappointing because I wanted it to be sweet and found it acrid like a knife. I gagged.

If you gag while giving head, if you vomit back the semen, chances are the fellow you are fellating won't be very kind to you. That was an afternoon of firsts, including a black eye and a split lip.

What few friends Wiggins had left in the world bring him to a retired Watson and his new Missus. Wiggins's wounds are tended, he is bathed, they give him clean clothes and a bed in a room facing the east so the sun could reach his bruised and swollen face. Through the morphine Wiggins would have dreams about Holmes, who has let death come between them.

My disfigured Wiggins is visited by Sherlock's older brother Mycroft. Wiggins is still bleary from opiates and has trouble taking in all of Mycroft. The man is immense. Only his tailor would know his exact proportions—a state secret. Fat men are as common to Victorian literature as ghosts and small glasses of sherry. Their size is not reprimanded by such authors as E.F. Benson or Henry James.

We have never met but I know you. Mycroft wears a shoddy overcoat. His indiligence is often mistaken as thrift. *If I belonged to another family, I might say that my brother spoke about you highly. But the true of the matter is that Brother Sherlock never mentioned you once. His colleague set down your name on rare occasion. One of the little flies on the wall.* Mycroft is winded and his gaze often strays to the bed where Wiggins has been convalescing. *I have my reasons to believe that your skills may help solve another crime. I'm not my brother, I have different rules and aims, and greater resources at my discretion. I'm not talking a guinea in your pocket, boy. Comfort is within your reach.* They stare at one another, each practical yet unable to comprehend what stirs in the attic of the other's mind, until the moment becomes intolerable. *I know you can nod,* Mycroft says.

My story of Holmes's survivors requires mystery. There has been a murder at a most private dinner club Mycroft belongs to and he needs Wiggins's help solving the crime.

I've never written a mystery before. And my sleuth cannot speak because he lacks a tongue, cannot read or write because he was a street urchin. This is not encouraging. I begin to wonder why I shouldn't take the easier path and write a simple romantic tale. Why be undone when I could offer readers Wiggins and Holmes, homosexual affairs forbidden by law during their day, intergenerational affairs forbidden by law still in our day? Shouldn't the taboo appeal to me?

It doesn't. I miss the deadline.

MONTHS LATER I AM INVITED to submit to another anthology. I revisit poor Wiggins and create the Club Tarrare. Its door once belonged on the stables of Jean-Baptiste Colbert's mistress but came to London because the fattest men in the capital demand something both wide and eminent for the entrance to their gentlemen's club. It opened by pulleys and gears. Mycroft and Wiggins stand there and gaslight illuminates the owner and fabled chef, the twin brother of Henri de Toulouse-Lautrec, who works with sauces rather than paint, menus rather than lithographs. This brother Purvis is even shorter than his artist twin and is not at all pleased to see Mycroft has brought someone so thin to the club.

The older men speak French for a while. Wiggins listens to the terse tones of their argument.

On your knees, boy, the dwarf tells him in English.

Wiggins looks up at Mycroft who nods.

There, on the soiled cobblestones, Wiggins kneels. His left side trembles as the memory of being beaten and disfigured threatens to overcome him.

Open your mouth. The dwarf reaches out to clutch Wiggins's chin. The dwarf's breath smells sickly-sweet, like rotten fruit.

Wiggins does as the dwarf commands. A thumb invades his mouth. The dwarf peers inside. *A Msr. Dudley once asked me what might be the rarest meat I had ever tasted.*

Wiggins bears the indignity. He has no interest in the answer and is not the least bothered when none is forthcoming.

He is two stone heavier than the others, but I am satisfied, the dwarf says before turning back to the club. *Since he will work for free.*

The air wafting from the open doorway is scented with orange. Tonight's many courses all feature oranges as a primary ingredient: smelts from the Medway baked in beurre blanc sauce; cotelettes de Perdreaux à la Duc de Chartres; hare à la Macgregor; sauce au jus de Bigarades. Eels. Sweetbreads. Oysters. Everything floating in orange juice, candied in rind.

Along with the power of speech, Wiggins has lost all interest in food and eats to live as opposed to Mycroft, who lives to eat and has saliva filling his mouth. The most powerful man in the British Empire is ready to fall to his knees for an entrée, such is Toulouse-Lautrec's culinary prowess.

Mycroft is a bully, though. As was his brother, who had a tongue like a knife. Mycroft enjoys using intimidation in affairs of state. He demands that the chef hire Wiggins as a servant. All of the staff working the Club Tarrare are either dwarves or emaciated so that patrons can feel more gargantuan—none weigh less than three hundred pounds. There are no normal mirrors in any of the club's many rooms but there are looking glasses fashioned originally for American carnivals that offer reflections that stretch a man wider.

Wiggins has agreed to help Mycroft not out of debt or even for pay. He is scarred and hopes that solving the murder mystery will distract him from his wounds. In the club's servants' quarters, he shares a room with a man dying of stomach cancer. The physicians of 1891 are unaware of mesenchymal tumors. Robbie Ostroff died of gastric cancer one hundred years later. His wife was at his hospital bedside. She never enjoyed performing fellatio on Robbie and had no idea that once a fifteen-year-old boy had given him head or that Robbie had contracted chlamydia twice in college.

Wiggins's dying roommate has worked the club for over a year and smokes so many cigarettes that his fingertips are yellowed. He warns Wiggins that pouring sherry and brandy and placing plates before diners are not the only tasks Toulouse-Lautrec expects of his staff. On the third floor are a number of chambers like no other in London. If a plump patron can withstand the duress of two flights of stairs—and the banisters are scarred from fingernails digging deep like the rock face of mountains suffering the bite of pitons—he can enjoy immense bathing tubs, Egyptian cotton sheets on round beds with goose-down pillows. And lovers.

For reference, I think of a more sophisticated version of the fraternity house I pledged in college. I weighed 110 pounds at the time, the scrawniest freshman to rush Zeta Psi. My ribs were visible when they would make us strip down to our boxers for hazing. I discovered later that my pledge nickname was to have been Auschwitz but a second black eye from yet another indiscretion saved me. I was Pip, like the mark on a die. Or *Great Expectations*.

All the pledges had to serve dinner to the brothers. Actually, we were not supposed to refuse any request made of us lest it jeopardize our enrollment at university or hurt the fraternity.

One brother was a theater major. He was soft-bodied smooth, with a mop of auburn hair. I watched him play Falstaff twice. I was charmed twice. He lived at the fraternity house and I knew his schedule enough to be present when he might shower before bedtime. He saw me stare at his dick and balls, hanging loose from the hot water, and told me I had to blow him. The fraternity was homophobic (it was the late eighties) and had already expelled a pledge they suspected of being gay, *so this could only be a test*, I thought.

WIGGINS BECOMES THE FAVORITE OF a patron, of course. Perhaps a scene with him helping out of the bath a large man.

Good lad. The room's a bit chill. Fetch me a towel? Kind of you not to ask about the knee. The fair sex is not the least bit fair when it comes to afflictions of affluence. Gout might as well be French pox. Oh, I shouldn't be maligning the French ... that toad listens from behind the walls, I heard more than once. (louder) *No price too steep for this feast.* (softer) *Could you help dry my legs? That knee makes it intolerable. Good lad. Seen but not heard is a gratifying manner.*

I read E.F. Benson to immerse myself in the world of Victorian social climbers and manners. Benson wrote a good many ghost stories, several of which have a measure of homoeroticism. And I learn from Brian Masters's comprehensive biography that Benson was attracted to men, was friends with Oscar Wilde before his trial, but may have died a virgin. He found the idea of carnality to be distasteful, beastly. He would be considered asexual now, I suppose, if his thoughts on sex were not solely self-loathing due to morality.

Sex as beastly. The beast with two backs. I write in the margins of Masters's book all sorts of notes. Some for the story, some for myself. The days when I felt attractive are gone. Is this due to self-loathing or has age culled my libido?

I cannot decide if the man that Wiggins helps from the bath is the murderer or the next victim. My enthusiasm for the mystery falters every day I read what I have written.

If Mycroft is as smart as Doyle wrote him, then Mycroft should have deduced the solution without even needing Wiggins present. Unless he has an ulterior motive, which stymies me.

I miss another deadline. Another anthology.

TESTOSTERONE BRINGS ME BACK TO Wiggins and the Club Tarrare.

I weigh more than twice what I did in college. I'm more than twice as old, too. My hair is graying but is still thick. I have, I often think, too much hair. My shoulders, my chest, my back, my arms, my stomach, my ass. I've become a bruin. When my doctor wonders why I have not had sex in a decade, he schedules me for blood tests in case I have low testosterone—a condition briefly seized by pharmaceutical companies as a chance to sell various topical hormones, until men using the drugs started dropping dead from heart attacks. The fraternity Falstaff passed away from a heart attack last week, by the way.

I was researching testosterone and came across the case of Charles-Édouard Brown-Séquard, a scientist who was a pioneer in endocrinology ... and injected himself with an elixir prepared from the pureed testicles of guinea pigs, dogs, and monkeys in the belief it would help with his impotence. 1889. Mad science. Two years before my story. Mycroft would have heard of Brown-Séquard, perhaps even attended one of his lectures at the Royal Society.

Mad science. Elixirs. Mysteries do not intrigue me but the strange and fantastical do.

By 1891, five years have passed since another notable scientist Mycroft would have been familiar with committed suicide: Henry Jekyll. A wonderful essay by Carolyn Laubender suggests *The Strange Case ...* is a gay allegory if not Jekyll's attempt to concoct a solution that would rid himself of his sexual inversion. The character of Enfield suggests that Hyde is blackmailing Jekyll and one of the more common reasons men of a certain station were blackmailed was threat of revealing their homosexual affairs. None wanted to follow the fate of Oscar Wilde.

I'm excited to write sentences including Enfield, how he discovered the formula among Jekyll's effects but as a layman could not make sense of the constituents. He knew it had value, though, and kept it safe somewhere hidden. Perhaps Mycroft has yet to uncover where? Five years of too much food and drink, of gout and diabetes, and a bloated Mr. Enfield can no longer enjoy the pleasures of women like once he had. Brown-Séquard's experiments were known as an utter failures and made him a laughingstock. But Enfield and Mycroft knew of a treatment that did bring out the beast in a man. Beasts think of two delights: feasting and fucking. Hyde would have terrified E.F. Benson. Benson should have drank a gallon of the formula, I think. A portly man with a thick mustache damp with virility.

The mystery of deaths at the club now seems a ploy of Mycroft, something villainous to secure the elixir because what Empire doesn't have a need for mad science? Wiggins is a dupe, though. How can he seduce anyone? How can I seduce anyone these days?

The story is impossible to finish. I have abandoned "The Case of the Club Tarrare."

Yet I know my ending: *Wiggins holds the vial. So little, not enough to share with Mycroft. The elixir looks as clear as gin but coats the glass sides like treacle. His removes the cork and the smell is stringent and raises the hairs on his neck. He tips his head back. The first drop stings the old wounds of his mouth, pools in the pit where once was a tooth and Wiggins shudders as he feels something stiff and sharp lance through his gums. A new ivory incisor. If just a trickle returned the tooth then his tongue—*

IT HAS BEEN SO LONG since last I had a man in my mouth that I can no longer remember the taste and so I find myself unable to type the words that need to happen to end the mystery without lying to myself. As I have so often done. I never dared unzip Robbie Ostroff; I was too scared at fifteen to even touch another guy, let alone taste him. And I turned away after Falstaff's offer, fearful that he would tell if I reached out and, scared, so scared of what would happen, what my life would be like if he let me.

I'm more cowardly than Benson or Jekyll. I have found myself slowly transforming into a lumbering hulk, a hairy beast that is afraid of its appetites, ashamed of what it wants to consume. Am I too large for even the mirrors in the Club Tarrare?

Wiggins, please regain your tongue and tell me that everything will be all right.

PASSION, LIKE A VOICE
— THAT BUDS

THE ANCIENT THERMOSTAT NEARED NINETY but I hid from summer as I had from the rest of the year: rarely leaving my apartment, able to count on the fingers of both hands the number of times I had opened the door or even a window in each of those twelve months of dim light and silence. No television. No speakers for the computer. No calendar.

My father would have used the word calidity. Calidity, my father's first impressive word.

Perhaps it was an eager July, perhaps a contrary September—Philadelphia knew both. If I lay in bed trying to read or sleep, I would have the air-conditioning on but the sheets still clung to my sweaty, bare skin. If I was restless and went through the rest of the apartment, I might linger beneath the laboring unit in the living room a while. I was retired but not yet sixty, no gray straying past the wispy facial hair that grew unattended, able to stay alone without work not from Social Security but disability.

That day, somehow an immense wasp had found its way inside my apartment. It looped around the apartment before returning to the window. I tugged on the cord to raise the blinds slowly. I did not want to injure my new guest, which had an hourglass waist any woman, by birth or design, would envy.

But watching it seek a way out of my stifling apartment gave me small comfort. My life had been reduced to increments. Tiny pleasures, awareness of minute threats. Micrograms of venom are enough to enrage neurons, erode the walls of cells. Or a virus that plays hugger-mugger with my body's immune system. No, the wasp was a welcome distraction from the death building inside me.

The clocks' second hands were a staccato beat that lulled. I once danced in *discothèques* in New York, Philadelphia, even Montreal. Over the years I had acquired enough analog clocks to keep every room aware of the time. Even my bath, though I never glance up at the clock face, a jaundiced man-in-the-moon with an old-time rocket ship plunged into one eye, a Victorian gentleman dangling by a cord as the pendulum.

Lately, I wonder if dying has brought an urgent clarity to my thoughts and knew I noticed the significance of details, their echo of greater and perilous things, or was my mind too sick? Ganglia like a spastic telegraph operator who has but one page of code to transmit over and over and …

To escape the wasp in the bedroom, I moved to the chair at my dusty desk and stared at the image on the monitor, the homepage loading an electron micrograph of the virus with the likeness of Eihort that infected me. Poor Lovecraft—his vision was clouded. Polyps weren't trying to invade our world from beyond the stars. They had already conquered mankind and inevitably lined the slimy walls of his intestines.

A chime sounded a new email to an old address that I could not bring myself to shut down. Though it had been over three years since the last issue of *Rugose* saw print, still I would receive queries and submissions. How can poets be optimists? Or perhaps I misread the emails—I actually had not opened any in months, just clicked and marked them as read—and they were acts of desperation. A poem as plea, a line as poorly worded as, "I haven't seen your face before, would you like a drink?" or "You've lost so much weight, I don't think that's a good sign." or "These days being positive isn't a death sentence."

I thought it odd to get a flurry of emails but the ding-ding-ding was louder. The doorbell. I creaked when I stood, winced as I walked across one room to the next, all dim, all too-warm, all windows shut, blinds drawn, save the one with its wasp.

I do not get visitors. My friends are dead, and acquaintances have been silenced by the wounds inflicted when I stopped calling, writing, acknowledging them. I only know of Monday, when a delivery boy brings ten prepared meals. A gesture of the day of the week, the miracle of MANNA or so the group's website says. Food does not interest me and most often the boxes inside the refrigerator become spoilt before I finish the lot.

The boy delivering the food disturbs me. My normally-feverish body might shiver whenever I ruminated on the words he said, the gestures he made, the implied overtures. I knew that as soon as I opened that door and let him inside my apartment, I would feel vulnerable. Animal predators look majestic in photographs and even in zoos from a distance, but when one is staring you down, only a fool admires it. He was like that. Beautiful and, because of his unfathomable interest in me, a risk.

Not that I feared he might rob me. I had little. They do not deliver meals to wealthy folk.

I did not think he would do me violence, either. But his interest in me could not be defined in anything that came close to healthy. I thought about ignoring him, leaving the door locked. Starving myself. I did not fear dying. After living with the virus for a decade, I'd been through all the stages of grief and settled into apathy. I think that my body, overripened to the point where the skin was discolored, spongy, offering nothing wholesome only poison, could not abide the company of a body half its age, ten times its vitality. No, what left me so anxious was that, in the span of just one month, he had come to know me so well that he used my first name, dropped any unnecessary rules of conduct, and managed to get me to eat a meal and talk about things I had not recalled or spoken of in a great many years. Meanwhile, all I knew of him was a name—Kearny, so unusual for anyone, I wondered if it might be his surname, but it did not sound Latino, and my Internet searches led only to the name of an upstate New Jersey town, pronounced the same as he did, Kar-nee, like carny, carnival workers without the best reputations— and the fact that he was enrolled in City College. But what year, what age, what reason for him volunteering for MANNA ...? He skillfully diverted any attempt to learn these simple facts. He seemed shy at first, but his last visit he was so charming that I realized he was flirting with me. Isolation makes coquetry unrecognizable until it becomes blatant. Or too late.

Yet, I would be remiss to not admit that some part of me was flattered.

As I turned first one deadbolt and then the other and called out—the first time I had spoken aloud today?—"Wait a sec," I worried what happens when the china shop delivers to the sick bull?

The bull that day was weaker than ever. I did not want to go to the hospital. I wanted to pass while sitting in a chair, like my father had when his lungs had become porous and hard and choked with phlegm. Hospice had given him liquid morphine for pain, but he passed in his sleep. Now I regretted sharing those tiny bottles at a horror convention, toasting a poet's recent Rhysling award for his rondeau about chthonians I published.

I suppose one could overdose on Truvada, but I did not want my suicide to be misinterpreted as a statement on Big Pharma. My name was once known enough to be mentioned on blogs for a day or so.

The cologne Kearny doused himself with masked any scent of the food in the paper bags he carried in both arms. I found the scent a bit astringent. My nose had once bled after he left and I breathed in his fugacity. I had stared at the droplets. Here, with these few drops, a plague held at the tips of my fingers.

He remembered the way to the kitchen and left me to close and lock the door.

I heard him set the packages down on the near-empty countertop, the rustle of paper and plastic, the opening of the refrigerator door.

"You're not eating," he called out.

"I only find within my bones, a taste for eating earth and stones," I said and walked into the kitchen. He wore a baby-blue tank top and jean shorts with the cuffs rolled back and tight against muscular legs. Matching pale blue socks with little pom-poms at the back, the sort a little girl would wear, accented his white sneakers.

"You need to eat." He lifted one packaged meal. "No carrots, like you asked."

I nodded.

"Why no carrots?" He wasn't looking at me when he asked, as if he was more curious about the limited contents of my refrigerator than my limited diet.

Even as I began to answer, I realized he was emptying my past again. A hermit still likes to be asked why he became a hermit. A mute would love nothing more to tell what happened to his tongue.

"My mother was what they called a 'health nut' back in the day. She owned a juicer and almost any vegetable she could find at the supermarket went into that contraption. But mostly carrots. She believed all the tips in the slick magazines at the check-out lines that are as good as porn to homemakers. Recipes, advice. How to stay thin. How to stay happy. Healthy. She must have read that carrot juice was the healthiest thing to drink and a glass or two every day would ensure she did not end up like my father—"

"His lungs …" Kearny threw away the old food. Of course he remembered what I told him about my father.

"Yes. I forget the nutrient alphabet that's in carrots but the kitchen came to stink of them. And maybe if she was only drinking the juice it would be fine. Her skin did turn yellow-orange. Carotenodermia they call it. The doctors taught me that word. But so much juice and the vitamins and taking cod liver oil…she destroyed her liver. Outlived Dad by only two years.

"People don't want to read warning labels on things. They just rush ahead. If they took the time to read the warnings on diets… books …. Books can be dangerous. Boys, too."

He had a high laugh. "Do you have a warning label?"

"I do." I believed that somewhere in the apartment, among the papers, was my first and follow-up blood test results.

Kearny stepped closer. Too close. The air in the room, already warm, made doubly so from two live bodies in close proximity, became stifling. The tiles beneath my soles were no longer cool, could not offer me any relief from the calidity.

"You *especially* should have a warning," I said.

"Where would they put it?" He raised an arm, traced a line along the inside of the dark-skinned limb as if telling a tattoo artist where he wanted his ink.

"All over."

He smiled and nodded and surprised me—no, relieved me—by turning his back to me. He began searching the cabinets to find a clean plate and glass. "I'm going to fix your lunch and watch you eat it, so I know that one meal won't go to waste."

How much had I told him? From whom I had contracted the virus? (I didn't know.) How long had it been since I'd been with another man? (You were still crawling.) My father's obsession with words? (Began when he was waiting at the dentist's office and trying to finish an *Inquirer* crossword puzzle someone else had abandoned. An eight-letter word for "heat" flummoxed my father, who purchased his first newspaper the next day to learn the answer: calidity. The last three ponderous words he memorized were idiopathic pulmonary fibrosis.) Why I loved poetry? (Reciting poetry alone in my room as an anxious teen was like an incantation, an invocation from harm. Abracadabra.)

I sat down at the small table and watched him. Displays of domesticity exhausted me. I dusted and cleaned only when a sense of shame rose in my throat.

A small carton of two-percent milk helped me swallow the dry whole wheat English muffin. I poked the flimsy eggs, so yellow, a false note of cheer that became depressing when lifted dripping on the tines of my fork.

I noticed his tank top was splashed from the overactive spigot. He turned the chair around and rested his chin on the back and watched me.

"I wonder if you spend so much time on the rest of your delivery route."

He shook his head—well, more wiggled it back and forth.

"I'm not your only—"

Again, the smallest of gestures.

"Your shallow tongue-talks at tables …."

He slipped a hand behind him. The hip flask was small, thin, curved as if meant to hug his ass. The metal scratched and even dented as if to say, a sloppy drunk owns me. I erupted into a fit of giggles and had to cover my mouth.

He frowned. I begged an apology. "I don't think I've ever known anyone who carried one of those. I thought they were Father's Day gifts, like ties covered in trout, and never taken out of the drawer."

His fingers spun the cap off with accomplished ease.

"Are you even old enough to legally drink?"

As usual, he ignored my question and poured until the upturned cap was full of clear liquid. Like a girl playing tea party, he elevated his pinkie when he tipped the cap into his mouth.

The second capful he offered to me. Whatever the liquid was, it tasted like the Atlantic Ocean.

He drank another. So did I. A noticeable tingling sensation at my fingertips and my chapped lips made me tilt the empty cap towards him. He responded by pouring more.

"It's been a long time since I—"

"You've never had this before."

"Oh? How do you know?"

"It's an orphan drug," he said.

"So then we must be orphans to drink it? Or to enjoy it?"

He wrapped a hand around my own, adding his temperature to the tingling, but only for a few heartbeats before he took the cap from me and screwed it back onto the flask.

"You're kind of ripe."

Like old fruit. I had run out of deodorant last year and never saw the need to buy more. I had grown accustomed to my body odor. When you rarely speak, a deep inhalation of your armpits is a sign you're still alive.

"And your cologne reeks."

"Being clean would make you feel better," he said.

"None of us are ever clean on the inside."

"True. When was the last time you showered?"

"More questions. I'll take a shower if you answer ... I mean, really answer, one of my own."

He lifted his arms wide and sat back as if doing so made him look vulnerable. "Ask me."

"Do you know what a bugchaser is?"

"So you think you're a fetish to me?"

"That's not an answer. But yes." There were times when I ached to indulge in one of my past petty vices. A cigarette. A drink. Either gave me something to do with my hands, allowed me props to yield the perfect pause when talking to another guy. Plastic fork and knife held no promise to make me look refined. More geriatric.

"I don't think most folk understand the risks or rewards to any indulgence. Satisfied?"

I shrugged. When I stood up, he put a gentle hand on my upper arm and guided me toward the bathroom, but he stopped while walking past my PC, still on.

"What's that?"

The screensaver on the computer monitor captivated him. Two images side-by-side. Electron microscopic HIV molecule. The second, an Erol Otus rendition of Eihort from the *Call of Cthulhu* game.

"It's an artist's rendering of a monster."

"Oh? From, like, a movie?"

"No, actually a short story. Written in the 1970s by an English kid. It's called Eihort and is found underground. People come to it, and it demands they make a bargain."

"So, they sell their soul to it, like the Devil."

I shook my head. "No, actually the bargain is a terrible one. If they accept it, they get infected by one of Eihort's children, tiny creepy-crawlers. That do nothing but multiply until they kill the host and scurry out of his hollowed-out body.

"And if the person refuses, Eihort just smothers them with its bulk."

"That's the stupidest thing," Kearny said. "Why would anyone take such a lousy deal?"

"As I said, it was written by a kid. And supposedly anyone who seeks Eihort out is insane. Sort of like anyone who would willingly infect themselves with HIV."

I had covered the mirror in the bathroom with the torn covers of paperbacks I had once bought from Darrel Schweitzer. I do not need to see myself. I have become a forgotten still life in a Joe Brainard poem. I close my eyes. I see old fruit.

The Méliès moon watched me. I lifted a hand to block its view. The surviving eye winked between my fingers.

"I don't hear the water running," Kearny said. It's one of the most domestic statements known to man, a line that has been uttered since mankind invented the shower and if not for this new energy inside of me I would feel weary at having a young man talk to me so.

He stepped into the open doorway and trembled. We stood there, trembling and staring at each other, like participants at a St. Vitus Day dance. And he reached out, arm stretching before my eyes to tug the shower curtain open and I stared at the skin of his arm, marveling at the tone, the muscle, the sheen.

I stepped into the tub. He followed and turned the tap.

First he removed my t-shirt, then fumbled with my sweat shorts as beneath them were boxers I had worn for the last few days. They puddled in the rising water at the base of the old tub. I stepped back, under the spray

142

and nudged the drain switch so the water would travel down the pipe rather than up and spill out. If my evident boniness bothered him, he did not say. My penis was not quite limp but neither did it raise its head like a dog eager for a pat, accompanied by cooing.

He stripped off his tank top. His bare chest looked far different than I expected. Several ribs and sternum had grown abnormally, allowing a trough between his nipples. As if some organ had been removed without the aid of a scalpel or sutures and left this sunken appearance as a reminder. He shucked his jean shorts next. He had not been wearing underwear. He did not have anywhere close to the unruly public hair I had allowed to become pungent brambles. No, he had reduced his pubes to thin fuzz from which his uncircumcised penis hung as did a surrounding cluster, an assemblage of growths. Those farther away from his limp sex were no larger than nipples and the same color as his skin, but many, so many, were sprouts and wens the size of a child's pinky, yet with a cauliflower tip instead of a nail. As he brought my hand down to grasp his penis, the growths brushed my wet skin. He took hold of my penis. "Safe safe we're being safe," he whispered into my ear. I heard the syllables trying to merge into a mantra.

If not for the elation I'd imbibed, I would have taken two glances, decided the poor boy has a terrible outbreak of genital warts, and push him away. But the salty drug had trickled down the folds of my brain and watered the old memories with the thinnest of roots. I was not in Philly, but in the Louisiana, twenty years old, a college sophomore, a pledge out at night. Not New Orleans, but maybe a small town. The memory of where was less than what: we had to buy something at an all-hours convenience store. Alcohol, maybe, or snacks, to bring back our fraternity's brothers. The guy behind the counter was fat, a word too kind, too small. Perhaps he was nowhere as obese as my memory wanted him to be. Ginger-haired, too, but balding. So many pink flesh tags covered every inch of exposed flesh, his pink trotter arms, his wrinkled neck, his face, his forehead, his cheeks, his chin, his eyelids. Hundreds and hundreds of skin tags peduncled him. We stared at him like country bumpkins at a freak show ready to hand over our money. We dropped the sweaty bills for whatever it is we bought—booze, snacks, as if it mattered—into his palm and would not take the change. We were terrified that whatever skin condition he had might be contagious.

I never remembered to ask any of the doctors I had seen since what the fat man might have had. But I remembered him when I saw the countless twisted legs on Otus's Eihort, a pale, boule de suif with many eyes. And the spikes on the HIV molecule. Nature had outdone Lovecraft, had brought Campbell's nightmares to life.

So I map excrescence. / I probe its twisted fibres till I find / The core of its cabala, in my mind.

Because of the memory, I could not ejaculate despite Kearny's frantic tugging. He gave up when the water went cold on us.

The liquid euphoria had passed. I would piss it out soon. I collapsed on my bed. Not so different from yesterday, only the sheets clung to skin damp from water rather than sweat.

I turned and watched him stand naked in front of the sink. He tore away the papers blocking the mirror and looked at himself. He opened his mouth, perhaps checking his teeth, his tongue.

He retched. Over the bathroom sink. A long series of coughs and heaves that did nothing good to his torso or my self-esteem. Retch had onomatopoeia. Boys, boys, boys. From the retching and the spewing of the boys.

I thought I heard a small *plunk* as whatever he brought up landed near the drain.

He turned and wiped his lips. He went to my dresser and searched until he found an undershirt that time and cheap detergent had left gray. The growths, his penis, sagged as he slipped the fabric over his chest. Then he took a pair of equally discolored underwear and slipped them on.

"There's a wasp on the window," he said.

"I know."

"Do you want me to kill it?"

It seemed a cruel act. Some things just find themselves in unfortunate bedrooms. "No. It will die eventually."

"From starvation?"

"Or the heat. Remaining on the window pane would be like lying on a griddle. Insects don't sleep but they go into torpor like gay, old men do. Some insects never eat. Cicadas. Mayflies. I don't think they have mouths."

"Cicadas have to have mouths," he said. "They make those sounds."

"No. Their wings. Frantic beating. All to find a mate. They only make the sounds to find a mate."

He sat on the edge of the bed and reached out to stroke one of my bare legs but I moved away from him.

"Next week," he said. Promise? Threat? Did it matter?

After he left I turned off the air-conditioning and lay in the dark and waited for the room to become an oven. In the silence, I heard a skittering, slushing sound from the bathroom. Something crawling on the dingy, wet tiles. I rolled to the edge of the bed. Something pale crawled to the edge of the room. A ball composed of four or five fat, wide-eyed grubs, maybe.

Then came the buzzing of wings. I looked at the ceiling, the wasp looping, excited. It did one more lap around the room before it dive-bombed the grub-thing. And they began a tango that resembled love but would end in death for one. For both, I suppose, as what purpose did either have but to sting and breed? Sting and breed.

HIS MOUTH WILL
TASTE OF CHERNOBYL

PLEDGES ARE NOT PERMITTED TO walk up the steps to the front porch and walk in through the front door of the fraternity house. We have to enter through a small side door and do so one at a time, each answering a question posed by the brother inside; we're segregated because every day we're told pledges are just three-fifths men until we reach initiation. Last night it rained—it's always raining warm water in New Orleans, but this city never smells clean—and I stood outside, getting soaked, as Carl recited the hometowns of every brother. Tonight, I'm asked how many chapters of Zeta Psi there are (eighty-eight, which also happens to be the atomic number of radium, decaying and toxic radium—being a pledge is often a tiresome meme brought to life).

My unease at being asked an easy question grows as they herd us, not into the living room as so many times before, but before the bar. The mirrors behind the bar are stained with age, and my reflection looks sick.

Noble, the pledge master, is behind the bar. He's chipping away at a bag of ice with a steak knife. "So, how are you all today?" His tone is less than sweet. Some guys don't know how to be kind.

"Fine," we all say at once like we're in first grade rather than freshmen at college. I try and make the syllable sound enthusiastic, but I want to be elsewhere. I don't belong here.

New Orleans lured me then lied to me. My father spoke as if the city had been a sweetheart of his. He loved his alma mater more than my mother. I find the entire state stifling like the shacks at summer camp, when I discovered, surrounded by other boys, how much I wanted to push one into a dark room, form a knot with our limbs, take kisses. And afterwards the boy cried and as I wiped at the tears with my thumb; he told me he felt shame for what we'd done.

"So you've been pledges for three weeks now. Not quite halfway finished. I bet you're pleased with yourselves." And he stabs down hard so the knife remains vertical in the ice. His t-shirt is wet, maybe with water, maybe with sweat.

I can smell anxiety leaking out of the other pledges' pores.

"So if you're so fucking proud, tell me why then one of you was caught not wearing his pledge pin? On your very first day, we gave you those pins to wear ..." He taps his beefy chest with two fingers. "... to show you belong to us."

Confused, the other pledges look at one another. I know what happened. Noble's glaring at me.

I take a step forward. I'm not intimidated by any of them, especially not him. "I was in the shower—"

Noble takes a chunk of melting ice and throws it to one of the brothers lurking around us. "We said, 'Pins are to be worn at all times.'"

"I love how you boys are watching me at *all times*. The things you must want me to do—"

Noble grabs me by the arm. The brothers rush me. Topple me.

One holds my head against the floorboards, his hands so hot against my skin that the ice another brother presses against my ear is welcome. But I know what will follow. One of them tells me not to struggle, not to move or it will be worse. I swallow the bile rising in my throat. The ice doesn't numb the earlobe near enough and I feel the dull post of the pledge pin prick my skin. And I do struggle. The real pain begins the moment before the brother straddling me sucks in a breath—I hear each and every one of them, their heartbeats racing, their mouths panting like exhausted dogs—and a thumb presses against the cheap enamel on the front of the pledge pin. The metal post tears the delicate seam between earlobe and cheek. They offered a rag to bite down but I refused it; I saw one of them wipe down the sloppy bar with that rag. Instead, my teeth grind. I hear a brother curse being struck by my foot. I'm thrilled. The pain radiates out from my ear, to all the plates of my skull, to my jaw, and I'm sure the blood is trickling through the brother's fingers trying to keep my neck steady.

They have to push the pin through cartilage, they tell me, because I moved.

Before they release me, Noble says, "Now, Sippy, you won't forget to wear your pin again." His face is close to mine; he's been drinking too much Malört and he might as well gargle dirt and turpentine; I close my eyes, which are tearing.

They nicknamed me Sippy after seeing my graduation gift: an heirloom silver hip flask, wrapped in butter-soft leather. I've come to refer to it as the Bailey flask.

On the night before my flight, my father took me to an expensive steakhouse in Philly. Both of us wore uncomfortable-looking suits and ties.

As my knife sliced off a glistening piece of fat from the porterhouse, he pushed the flask across the white tablecloth. My father doesn't wrap presents. "You need to take this with you. It's been in the family for generations. I took it to Princeton. Where you're going, you'll definitely need it."

The metal felt cold. Damp, also, so I wiped my fingers after picking it up. "No matching cigarette case? Or am I just supposed to be a lush?"

"With your vocabulary, I'm surprised you didn't score higher on the SATs." He took hold of my hand and pressed hard at the wrist bones. "Now listen to me. The flask will help you make friends. But you are never to drink from it. Ever."

I didn't wince then; my tolerance for pain has grown over the years. "Yes. Taboo. There's an SAT word for you."

"Doubtful." He let go of me. "Don't hesitate to offer someone a drink. Use the flask. It's how I met your mother."

And because I wanted to look like I had money in the bank, even if it was only my father's money, I did. During Rush week, when I offered it to one of the Zeta Psi brothers, they turned my kindness into a game of keep-away, laughing at me as they passed the flask back and forth between them. I cursed them all and during the walk home I anticipated the conversation with my father. But the next day, when I went back to the house, they greeted me as if I belonged, returned the flask with mocking ceremony, and invited me to pledge.

On my feet, I wipe my eyes with one hand. Someone snickers because of my tears; one of the brothers jokes that he's surprised my ear wasn't pierced already. *Ha ha, we're allowed to make homophobic remarks because we can't be that bad if we're allowing someone gay to rush us.*

"Let him go clean up."

The other four pledges surround me, like cavalry too late to the battle, their faces long, their eyes not meeting mine, because they have their pledge pins sticking out of their shirt collars or at their chests, over their hearts, not crudely thrust into an ear.

The bathroom on the ground floor of the fraternity house is dank, grimy, every corner moldy, and doesn't fit two people well, but Carl follows me inside, both of us too large for the pane of glass askew over the sink. I see that my ear is red with blood. I'll need it stitched. Or maybe glued. I have a cousin who used glue instead of bandages.

"Fuckers," I spit into the sink. The froth lands on a bit of dried shaving cream and hair.

"All you need to do is impress them. And then they'll forgive and forget." Carl turns the cold tap.

"Do *you* keep your pin clenched between your teeth when you shower?"

I peel off my shirt. The top bar of the Tulane *T* is ruined with bloodstains. And I snag my ear, which rekindles the pain, and begin yelling and cursing and trembling. Carl helps by calming my flailing arms, takes the wadded ball of shirt and holds it under the tap, presses the whole against the raging side of my head.

"None of them ever interrupted me showering. But from now on, yeah, we all will." He always talks with a cautious manner; otherwise I would think he's suggesting I'd welcome the intrusion.

I look pathetic. The dirty mirror is not flattering. I feel both ridiculous and remorseful. Carl is the ideal pledge; after three weeks he has yet to earn a single demerit, has nearly all the brothers' autographs in his book, has memorized both "In Flanders Fields" and the Greek alphabet backwards. He yearns to be a Zete. I think he believes that fraternities are just like treehouse clubs for college students, friendly and fun. I pledged because my father's college ring, with the golden letters Z and Ψ set in onyx, outlasted his wedding band. He'd stop the checks to Tulane if I didn't endure initiation.

After a rapping on the bathroom door comes, "Sippy, come on out!" and, "What are you boys up to in there?"

Carl frowns. I don't think he's gay. He told me he thinks one of his uncles might be and that he's bothered that neither of his parents talk to the uncle at all. Carl has manners, is the least selfish person I know. He doesn't stare, he doesn't snap, but smiles. Carl would be the good son in any family. I suspect my father would prefer Carl to me, and I should hate him for this, not because it makes any sense but because people think complete nonsense.

Catcalls greet us when we walk out of the bathroom. I flip the brothers the finger. I expect a few demerits for that gesture.

Noble must have wrestled in high school, those must have been *good years* he doesn't want to forget, because he never looks relaxed: he bounces on his feet when he stands and speaks, he often stretches his arms as though working out the kinks before lunging. His hair is buzzed to a sharp edge, which looks severe when he stands near Carl, who has black curls prone to tangling when he sweats. Noble's nose is thick, at odds with his smooth jawline. I wonder if he kept the uniform, if it hangs at the back of his closet. "Sippy, where's your pledge pin?"

I take the shirt away from my ear. "Here, sir."

"And your cup, Sippy?"

All the brothers love the conceit of the flask, so I have to carry *that* with me every day, too. I slide it out of my back pocket. "Right here, sir, warmed by my ass." A lie, actually, as the Bailey flask never gets warm. None of the other pledges gives lip to the brothers. And every time I raise my chin, meet their eyes, and offer a snide remark, the others wince, anticipating abuse.

Noble laughs. The slap of his right hand against my face stings, but nowhere hurts as much as my ear. But the humiliation makes me nauseated, my legs weak, my arms bereft of purpose. I don't want him to touch me again. I have to lean against Carl and hope that none of the brothers notice.

The Bailey flask thankfully distracts Noble. He unscrews the cap and sniffs the odors of hometown bars. "My favorite. You thought ahead. Very good, pledge."

But I'm neither mindful nor attentive. It's the flask, filling up with whatever its holder craves most.

My love for chemistry began with magic tricks: in junior high school the science teacher turned worthless pennies to silver and gold, created a cloud in a bottle, and started a fire with water. But nothing I've seen before compares to the flask. It should hold six ounces. I've seen it pour and pour and pour even more and it only makes sense when you're truly drunk.

Noble is from Chicago and boasts about the local schnapps, Malört. I'm told every semester he brings back to school a couple bottles. No one else *willingly* drinks it; the brothers make the pledges stomach the awful shit, which tastes like toffee scraped from the floor of the men's room, and lighter fluid, and rye bread burnt and metallic from the toaster.

Noble smirks, shoves the flask at one of the other pledges, and adopts a little girl's falsetto. "Drink me." And the boy does not hesitate to accept the flask and take a sip, because we must do what they tell us. We have no choice. Being a pledge means never refusing whatever they ask of you. We are told every day of the wonderful reward awaiting us ... as long as we always say yes.

And because the pledge wants to please Noble, the flask remains full of Malört. Except for me. I'm the only pledge that can say no to him.

WE'RE DISMISSED AT TEN O'CLOCK. Before we leave, Ross, the fraternity president, stops me by casually pressing fingers against my bare chest. He has a nickname but none of the pledges can address him by it, has no neck, and his face looks like he's eaten a ghost pepper. "Sippy. Go to the med center. But remember a steady house is built on tight lips."

I struggle to keep from laughing at Ross. The time to be afraid I would walk into the provost's office and say I was hazed was gone the moment they tackled me. I nod in agreement, of course.

On the walk back from Broadway Street, where most of the Greek houses are, to campus, the other pledges worry over having to have their pins on them at all times. They glance at my ear, they mutter, they whine, they ask me again and again to tell how I was found by Noble, who wanted to surprise me with a 6:00 a.m. inspection before classes began. We were warned of the pins' burden when the brothers pressed them into our hands, but now the other pledges look at the one in my ear, the ones pinned to their clothes, as if they are radioactive, cancerous.

"Your ear will get infected," one tells me. He puts an arm around me and pulls me in close, as if to examine the damage. I feel him brush his lips against to my neck as if he really is trying to kiss me there.

I'm so worn down I don't push him away.

He's the pledge who drank Malört. I can smell it on his breath, which is barely hotter than the night air.

His fingers grip my upper arm, slipping underneath the shirtsleeve. A fingernail scratches the tender skin, making me shiver.

"You're drunk." My mouth is so dry that the words come out less an accusation than an excuse for me to submit.

Drunk straight boys never know when to end their teasing, or when their teasing becomes my fault and thereby a temptation. I'm not even attracted to this one.

Carl separates us before I do something regrettable. Again.

"Go to bed," he tells the other pledges and shoves them away.

I follow Carl home. He shares the same dorm as me, but he lives on the third floor, while I'm on the second. At the elevator he asks me if I'll be okay.

I grimace as I remove the pledge pin from the curve of my upper ear. "Yes, sir."

"Don't do that."

I grin. Carl is such a good boy that I become overwhelmed at times with the urge to taunt him. And that makes me think I'm more like Noble than I ever knew, and that disgusts me. Maybe that's why Noble chose me.

I step out at the second floor, and before the doors completely shut, Carl sticks his arm in their path. "Why were you up so early today?"

"Huh?"

The doors open and doggedly try to shut again, but he won't let them close. "We have Anthropology Tuesdays and Thursdays at eight. But I thought you slept late on Wednesdays."

"When did you become my calendar?" The doors slide back and forth between us.

"Steve—"

"Sippy likes to get the early worm now and then." I lean in and press the buttons for the fourth and fifth floors. I wave goodbye to him.

My roommate Jairo is herding elephants across a savannah of wrinkled newspapers covering the dorm room's cheap carpeting. His brown arms are covered with wet paste as he applies another strip of paper to the downward trunk of one elephant between his legs. He looks up at me, must see the inflamed ear and starts to get up, but I shake my head and gesture for him to remain on the floor.

"I'm going for a new look," I say. "Battered chic."

"Were you disobedient?"

"I was stupid."

Jairo earned a scholarship that brought him from Costa Rica—I can't remember the town and don't even know the country's capital—to study environmental sciences. He carries himself with a confident straight-edge that guilts me into being extraordinarily ethical when around him. He's a vegan, so I can't bring myself to eat even pizza when he's there. He tutors Spanish for free, and ours is the only room that hasn't hosted the pothead down the hall and his stash of Purple Kush.

Jairo marches. He belongs to groups my father would never donate to, which makes me admire him even more, while feeling exhausted by his endless integrity. The elephant piñatas he's been working on the past few nights might be for a protest against ivory sales or campus Republicans, or both. I should know. A good roommate should know these things.

Of course, he thinks fraternities are terrible things, even if they do recycle beer cans and bottles.

I don't think he's wrong.

He moves the bucket towards me. "I'll listen while you help me."

But I'm not in the mood to confide in him any more than in Carl. I sit down across from him and dip a torn strip into the watery paste. "You know that raw flour can be as much a hazard as raw meat."

"Unlike your friends, I don't drink just anything put in front of me." Jairo adds to the elephant's round torso. His ragged t-shirt looks stiff in spots from spilt paste.

"They're not friends. Well, maybe one. I like him."

Jairo smirks. His eyeglasses begin to slide down and I push them up the bridge of his nose with a tacky finger.

"Don't say it."

He shakes his head. "Having a crush on a guy is probably the worst reason in the world to join a frat. Other than your father extorting you."

I grumble something about him and tree-hugging.

"I think I want to make these very American." Jairo stands and walks over to his desk, where he finds a rag to wipe his hands. "Keep working."

"Isn't it unlucky for the trunk to point down?"

"Mmmhmm." He carries back a pair of scissors atop a stack of salvaged magazine pages, all slick and sliding. Blues and whites and glossy reds. He cuts a page into many thin strips before efficiently curling each strip by pressing it against one blade of the scissors.

"Adult male elephants are solitary," he says. "A full-grown male can weigh around five or six hundred kilograms. And no, I won't abandon the metric system for you." He dips one end of the curled paper into the paste before securing it to the piñata's body. "The males are happy to roam about all by themselves. Unless it's mating time …."

"You think I should avoid other guys unless I want to fuck?"

"Maybe when you weigh six hundred kilograms. But I think there are some in your frat who should be kept at a distance."

The brothers hate the word "frat." We learned the first week that no one in a fraternity—or rushing one—ever abbreviates it, a show of disrespect. Every time I misspoke and uttered "frat," any brother within hearing distance would go to the nearest tap, fill a glass to the brim with cold water, and empty it with one toss, right at my face. By day five, if any pledge said "frat," we all were splashed. I can't stop myself from frantic blinking whenever I hear the word.

My phone giggles, the sound of a text message's arrival. There are several unread messages. We're not allowed to bring our phones in the fraternity house.

R we good?

R we?

We good?

I tap away. *My bloody fingerprint is on the phone now.* I'm curious if Noble will respond to that. I add: *Bastard.*

Got carried away. Sorry. R u hurt? We good?

"Do elephants ever get drunk?" I ask Jairo.

His laugh is a rumble, as if he has a stomach full of rocks. "Not in the wild. All the stories about elephants eating fruit that's fermented on the ground are just that. Stories. You know chemistry—it would take days for the fruit to really ferment, and any animal nearby would eat the fruit before then. And think how much alcohol something the size of an elephant would need to get drunk."

I answer Noble with *Yes sir.*

"Good. A drunk elephant would be a terrible thing. A drunk and horny elephant—"

"Would be a monster," he says.

I turn to Jairo. He stares up at me and adjusts his crooked glasses.

"I think your ear is bleeding again."

I look to see if I have any glue in the drawers of my desk. A crust of dried cyanoacrylate has dried unbreakably around the nozzle of the tiny tube. I grab scissors and a washcloth and walk down the hall to the communal bathroom.

I let the hot water steam the mirror and drench the washcloth. I wipe the glass clear and see in the reflection the back wall of the shower stalls.

Early this morning Noble woke me, ringing my phone again and again, until I answered. "Sippy, I'm bored." He couldn't speak the truth, that he wasn't bored but was restless and couldn't forget or forgive what he made me do two days ago in his bedroom. And this morning he waited for me in the bathroom—at an hour when no one else was supposed to be awake. I imagine you're not supposed to fuck in the communal showers.

He trembled as I pulled the curtain closed and turned on the water. And that's why I let him touch me: because I could see the fear in his eyes and it promised I'd be bathing in that hot fear rather than merely water. I thought it would make me feel better.

It didn't.

I won't ever forget the taste of his mouth, the Malört. Everyone calls him Noble, but to earn his signature—and each pledge must coerce or convince every brother to sign his pledge book—you have to learn the truth behind his name, how he challenged the fraternity brothers in his days as a pledge to a drinking contest, shot for shot, and not a single one could handle more than two tastes of Malört. The story goes that after the contest, his breath smelled so rank that the nearest brother vomited all over the bar, the beginning of a disaster. One brother after another succumbed to the inevitable rise of acid and bile, half-digested pizza, and too much liquor, and heaved until the atmosphere in the room was almost toxic: a Chernobyl that left part of the house uninhabitable for days.

Noble has dead molars, gums stained dark, and a tongue reminiscent of a fetal pig, pulled from a jar of formaldehyde, dissected in twelfth grade. Kissing him makes me gag, but he only wants to kiss at the very end, when he's close. I muffle his groans with my mouth over his. Thank God he is too scared to go down on me; I worry his tainted mouth would blister the skin of my dick, make my foreskin peel away.

After cleaning the wound as carefully and thoroughly as I can stomach, I snip the nozzle from the tube and squeeze a bead of glue on the hinge of my jaw. I hiss as I press the lobe against the raw sticky skin. The water in the sink is tinted crimson all the way down to the drain.

Back in the dorm room, Jairo has cleared the floor of elephants and their mess. The herd is drying on his desk. He's in bed reading a paperback. That's his before-sleep ritual. Mine involves the flask.

"What are you going to put inside the piñatas?" I ask him.

He folds the page he is reading. "Can't do candy—I worry the wrappers wouldn't make it to the trash bins. If they made biodegradable candy wrappers, that would be great. Maybe I'll just leave them all empty and be symbolic."

"People don't like being disappointed."

The Bailey flask is by my pillow. My high school senior project inspired the name. Students could research and present on anything that happened in New Jersey, tying it into history or culture. While reading old chemistry books, I found out about William J.A. Bailey and Radithor. Bailey was a Harvard dropout, but that didn't stop him from referring to himself as a medical doctor. He founded a company that sold amber glass bottles of water with a tiny bit of radium isotope with labels promising "Perpetual Sunshine." It was the Viagra of the 1920s—really, one filthy rich idiot drank a bottle every day for years to add some pep to his step and kick to his dick. When the man lost his jaw and died after a long and painful stay in the hospital, he was buried in a lead coffin because his corpse was so radioactive. Bailey's patent empire crumbled. The FBI eventually released the story that the Soviets found Bailey in Cuba, teaching at a medical school. He triggered Geiger counters and so they executed him as an American Cold War spy.

I think of all the people who wished that radium water would cure all their illnesses, solve all their problems. Science as a miraculous, magical cure.

As I push open the trapdoor at the top of the ladder, a moist, thick heat trapped within the attic overruns me. The outside daylight seeps through the oddly peaked roof, enough that I can find the dangling cord of a single bare bulb. One pull and I see the attic is really an unfinished elevated crawl space. By the time I worm off the last rung and onto the floor beams, my face feels like a windshield in the rain.

Carl climbs after me. The brothers ordered me to retrieve last year's Halloween decorations, but Carl volunteered to help. I almost wish he hadn't because there's not enough room in the attic for the two of us to move about comfortably. He ends up on his hands and knees beside me.

The cardboard boxes I brush with one hand are mottled with mold and coated with dust. I reach blindly into one box and pull out a cheap plastic devil mask, the scarlet streaked with thick crud.

"I hate Halloween," Carl says. His pained face is inches away from my shoulder. Dark crescents bloom under his neck, his armpits.

"No one hates Halloween. There's all-you-can-eat candy. Free candy."

He shakes his head like a thick-coated dog after a bath and the sweat flies in droplets. "My folks celebrated the 'harvest'—"

I hold the devil mask in front of my face. The bits of Carl I see through the cut-out eyes look miserable. "That sounds spookier—"

"It's just pathetic." Carl reaches out and lifts the mask off me. "I was ... quieter before I came here."

I cannot imagine a *more* reserved Carl. I wonder why he even likes me. Because he has to?

He frowns. "I never said the word 'fuck' aloud until I came here ...."

I can't help laughing. "I remember when they made us sing." Reciting silly rah-rah pep oaths and songs. "They can make us do anything." I don't want to remember Noble coming to me in the showers. Even though it was awful, my body will betray me. "I'm surprised your parents let you rush a fraternity."

"They don't know." He tries to shove aside boxes so there will be more room, but nothing budges. "Maybe I'll tell them at Thanksgiving."

I bite back asking if his parents know about his gay friend. I want him to be keeping me a secret. You only keep great and terrible things secret.

He wipes sweat from his forehead.

I take the Bailey flask out of my pocket and then roll onto my back— the creaking sound I hear may be rotten lumber or my vertebrae cracking— and try not to stare at the bare bulb hanging low, or else the filaments will create spots in my vision. "I'll trade families with you."

He answers with a brief laugh.

"I guess they like gays even less than trick-or-treaters?"

Carl picks up the mask and pulls the elastic cord around his head, adjusting so he can see. "Why are you even here?" His voice is low, muffled, silly, and not sinister. "After what Noble did—"

"You know what our devil did to me?" I tug on the mask's goatee.

"He goaded them on to pierce your ear. He struck you."

I feel relief he doesn't know everything I've let Chernobyl do to me. I feel like a slut.

"Why stay?" he asks. "Wouldn't you feel safer, happier, among other gays? Isn't there a student group you could join?"

"In high school my first—my only—boyfriend outweighed me by fifty pounds. He would dance on my feet. I'm not talking being clumsy at prom, but me, sitting on the sofa and when he came back from getting one of his dad's beers from the fridge, he would step onto the tops of both my feet and do a little two-step until I begged him to get off."

"That's horrible."

"I think horrible has become my type."

He shakes his head. "No wonder you want to trade families. Your father—"

"My father was disappointed that I couldn't get into an Ivy League school. He didn't laugh when I told him that Tulane was the Harvard of the South. He's paying for all this because I agreed to become a Zete. Like he was. If I go home, he'll test me. Just like the brothers do every day. Secret handshake, reciting the motto, all the bullshit that pretends to be liberté, égalité, fraternité."

He moves closer. "I'm sorry."

The apology is sincere. Carl can only be sincere. And sincerity is like make-up, making everyone look prettier, especially around the eyes.

I don't want him to catch me staring into those eyes, so I ask, "Want to see a trick?" I hold up the flask.

He nods and the devil mask slides up and down his face, making me chuckle.

"Here, take this. Close your eyes, think about what you're really thirsty for."

He holds the flask in both hands, almost as if praying.

"Now go ahead and drink."

He pushes the mask up so he can take a sip. "It's cold," he says, almost as a question. He swallows more. "Cold water. That's crazy."

"And that's magic."

He pours some out onto his palm and shows it to me, as if I need convincing he's telling the truth.

"Honest. The flask is magic. When you hold it, whatever you crave pours out. Though it doesn't work for me." *Not that I know what I want.*

He laughs at the trick, tilts the Bailey flask until he's convinced the flow won't cease. He pulls off the mask and lets cold water run down over his sweaty face. "This is amazing."

I watch as he crawls to me, and I hold a breath as he moves over me. The friction generated could power a thousand electric turbines, more than all the world's nuclear power plants. His head knocks against the light bulb and I am afraid it will break and shower hot glass over his tousled hair. I grasp a handful of his sweat-and-water-soaked t-shirt to pull him away, and he falls atop me.

His damp face slides past my own. I can smell the chemical tang of his deodorant and the sweet scent the shampoo has left on his hair.

"Carl, it's ... it's only a trick," I whisper.

He stares at me. "Steve ..." His face is so wet, and drops fall off his nose and chin to strike my skin, and my mouth is open like it's time to catch the first snowflake.

Then he presses his lips against my own.

He's not a good kisser. His tongue is kinda all over the place. Sloppy. And he's dead weight, pinning me down.

I open my eyes and watch him as my fingers peel at the back of his shirt. One goes high and strokes the sweat-slicked skin of his back, the other goes low and reaches past the waist of his jeans and grabs his ass through the cotton of his boxers. He moans into my mouth, a sound I've never heard him make, and I have to echo him.

Our crotches rub and I guide him to grind again and again. I move my face so I can nip his cheek, suck on his ear. He finds the saltiest part of my neck and just clamps his mouth tight there.

"Please," I mutter into his ear—not really sure what I am begging him to do. Or maybe I'm asking permission because my hand finds its way beneath his boxers. When I touch the furry cheeks of his ass, I feel him shudder. And knowing what he's doing is all it takes for me to soak my own underwear and jeans.

He remains atop me for several minutes. I rest my lips against his forehead and rub his back, and think back to what happened at camp long ago. I worry what will happen when he lifts off me.

There's no grace in moving about in the cramped attic. He rolls off me. He's out of breath yet winces and arches his back, and finds the flask beneath him. He hands it back to me.

"We should ..." He licks raw lips. "We better bring these boxes down. Just bring them all down."

"We can't go down there looking like this. *They'll know.*" I realize Carl has never ever thought about the shame you wear after sex—even if you still are dressed you have an aura, often tangible, breathable, of messing around. Messing around with another guy.

He stares off at the boxes. "Maybe there's something here we can hide ourselves with."

I reach out and touch the patch of skin showing from where his t-shirt has risen. "We're okay?" And moments after the words leave my throat, I remember that was what Noble texted me.

Carl nods. But his eyes are distant.

I realize he finally can be insincere.

CARL DOESN'T SPEAK TO ME on the walk back to the dorms. The other pledges notice how quiet he is and try to stir him with trash talk. They scheme how wonderful life will be once initiation is over and we're all brothers. Next semester *we* could be the ones making pledges do whatever *we* wanted. I glare at them. I want to claw my ear, make blood run, and mark each of their shirts with a line of gore. I'm glad when we part ways, but Carl's cold presence in the elevator hurts as much as the others' ruthlessness. In the elevator, I'm tempted to reach out to wipe his face, even though there are no tears. But I know that expression.

I knock my head on the door once before opening. I'm defeated.

Yet the plump, white elephant Jairo has left me on my bed makes me smile. He's not in bed or at his desk, so I can't thank him. When I lift it, I marvel at how fragile it feels. And I hear something rattling around inside. I trace the arc of the trunk with my finger—this one, which he made for me, turns up.

I could almost believe that anything could be magical.

The door opens and lets in the smell of Indian food a step ahead of Jairo, carrying paper bags. His mouth is full and when he says "Hello," his teeth are half-hidden by whatever seitan and stew he ordered. His shirt has stains.

"I adore my elephant," I say, and hug him before he can even drop a bag.

"I can smell you and I've got a mouthful of curry." But he's laughing as he pushes me away. "What is it with that frat that makes you reek?"

I sucked in a breath. "It's brought out the worst in me." I sniff at my shirt collar. I do stink. "How do you know if you're a horrible person?"

I remember the first time, when the boy cried because of shame. And when I wiped tears from that face, I swore I'd never see that expression again. It's the real reason I once dated someone who didn't know shame, only the sick pleasure of hurting me. Seems like I draw such boys like rotting fruit brings flies.

"When I say the word rainforest and you respond with parking lot."

"I'm serious."

"You're not a bad person," he says. "Just tell me what you did and we'll figure out why you feel so guilty."

"I've fooled around with ..." I collapse on my bed, then realize I'm probably soiling my pillowcase.

"With?"

I gesture meaninglessly.

"The guy you like, I'm hoping," Jairo says.

I groan. "Yes. But not just him. And I don't think any of them really wanted me to ..." I tumble off the bed and on to the floor, being melodramatic.

"Ah, I forgot I'm rooming with the gay Don Juan." He offers me a hand up. "Were you both drunk? In both cases, I mean."

"No …" I slip my hands into my jean pockets. One finds the chill metal of the Bailey flask. I don't remember even picking it up in the attic.

Jairo frowns at the sight of it. "Life is always better when we're responsible. And even being tipsy makes judgment harder." He takes the flask from me and puts it in the top drawer of my desk. "The real question you need to ask yourself is did you want them to be accidents."

"Some present." I shut the drawer. "I prefer your elephant." I remember the feel of the piñata. Though papier-mâché, it had more weight than the flask. "By the way, what's inside my elephant?"

He wipes his glasses on his shirt. "I'm not telling. You'll have to break it and see."

"I couldn't." The thought of hurting the elephant is unbearable.

Guilt makes sleep impossible. In the darkness of the room, I open the drawer and stare down at the Bailey flask. The silver is tarnished in spots, like its sheen is diseased.

I can't think of it as magic. More cursed. It must pour out my need to be loved. I remember how the brothers welcomed me back after that disastrous first night. A kiss on the neck from another pledge. Chernobyl. Carl.

AFTER CLASSES ALL PLEDGES MUST head straight to the fraternity house. But when I walk in, no one accosts me with a list of chores, or demands another recital from the handbook. The brothers move about in an odd stupor, sober but lost.

I don't see Carl. Or Noble. I find Ross in the kitchen, staring at the crowded shelves inside the rank-smelling fridge that sounds ready to die. "Sippy, guess you heard by now."

"Heard what?"

He takes an open bottle of beer from the door rack and gives it a sniff. "Carl wants to de-pledge."

Five pledges is a sorry number; when my father was a pledge, he was among sixteen boys. Of course that was Princeton, not Tulane, and the Zeta Psi chapter here are all losers. Fewer pledges means fewer active brothers, fewer fees, less of the gelt to pay mortgage and utilities. A chapter can die a slow death from initiating too few pledges. The loss of Carl, their favorite, reminds them how precarious their house of cards is.

"I didn't know."

"Noble's at his dorm room now trying to talk him out of it." Ross takes a sip of the beer and winces. "You don't happen to have your flask on you?"

I've been to Carl's room a couple times. He kept things simple, neat. He trounced me in several games of Scrabble because I couldn't find in his dictionary any of the words I knew from science classes.

The elevator doors are closing when Noble shoulders them open. His face is a patchwork of stubble and blotchy-skin. He looks as if he's been pulled taut, wrung dry, then thrown into the garbage. To be a pledge master is an honor, and losing even one of your flock can mean you'll never be given the role again.

"Sippy, just who I wanted to see." He throws a meaty arm around my neck. "You're saving me the trip. I was about to come get you. Time for another lesson in pledge unity. Carl is having second thoughts and we're both going up there to make sure he goes to bed wanting to be a Zete.

"Unless this is your fault, Sippy." He stabs at the third-floor button despite it being lit from my touch seconds earlier. "You didn't say anything to him, did you?"

"Nothing. I said nothing."

Noble smacks my cheek. "Of course. A steady house is built on tight lips." He then pushes my upper lip down against my front teeth with his thumb. "Some boys don't know the right thing to do with their lips. I don't want these lips to get anyone in trouble."

I loosen the emergency button and the elevator groans back to life. Noble continues to stand inches away from me, depriving me of personal space.

"Did he give a reason for quitting?"

"Nah. This happens every couple of semesters. A lot of freshmen aren't ready to live life without mommy or daddy to run home to when things get stressful."

We reach the third floor. "If you promise to stop the—" I pause as the doors open on the bloodshot eyes of a cluster of students, who shuffle to let us out. "—hazing …" I whisper the word. "I'll convince Carl to stay."

Noble smirks. "Sippy, I was there when you both climbed down the attic ladder. I know the look of wanktermath when I see it. You gays can't resist trying something with a straight guy. I get it."

"Chernobyl, I think your brain caught cancer from your mouth."

He grabs the flask out of my back pocket as we head down the hall. "You're smart to bring this. Alcohol does a pledge good."

"No!" But he easily evades my attempt to take the flask back.

He's barking laughter. "You make me miss high school."

I realize the only thing he'll understand is a threat. "If you don't give me the flask now," I say, taking two steps closer so I can speak low and slow for him. "I'll walk away. And I'll walk to the Dean of Student Affairs and tell them everything. There'll be no fraternity left standing for Carl to come back to."

Noble's eyes narrow. He looks ready to spit acid. "Do you even hear yourself? Do you want to see your jaw on the floor and find out if the Dean knows sign language?"

"The flask." I hold out my hand.

He uses it as a wedge to lift my chin higher and higher until I feel pain and am seeing the top of his head and ceiling tiles. "Why's this so important to you, Sippy?"

If he hears me claim the Bailey flask was magic, he'd laugh and take a drink to spite me—and then I'd have to deal with a besotted Noble pawing at me in front of Carl. Or, I can imagine him shoving the flask into my mouth, making me choke until I give in and drink. No, I need an explanation he'd understand. More so, approve.

"I put roofies in the flask."

Understand, approve, but not expect. "What?"

"Rohypnol. I ... a guy in my chemistry class sold me some. It's how I made guys more compliant."

His face goes through a quick change of expressions until it settles on a leer. "You smart son-of-a-bitch." He chuckles and gives me breathing room. "I had no idea you had the balls to do anything like that, Sippy."

"Great. You're proud of me. Now, can I have it back?"

"Oh, no, this is evidence. This is leverage." He shakes the flask as if admiring how the old metal still gleams. "I may even forgive you for dieseling me, when you start supplying me with the stuff."

How could I not expect Noble to reach new lows? And this lie is a patch that unravels quickly. Unless ....

"Buy it from me," I say. "Twenty bucks. That's all I want."

He considers a moment. Students pass us in the hall. I'm relieved Carl is not among them. He checks his wallet. "I have two fives and a—"

"Sold."

He stuffs the bills down my shirt. "There you go, frosh."

"And I relinquish, renounce, abdicate any and all claims to this flask," I say, my voice getting louder so that whomever might oversee magic in the world can hear me. "Agreed?"

The universe doesn't seem to acknowledge the change in ownership. Not even with a flicker of the overhead cheap fluorescent lighting.

He pushes me toward Carl's room. "Stop clowning."

Carl has a single room. The name tag the floor's resident advisor stuck to the door during move-in is still attached, though the edges have curled.

I knock two times on the door and call out to Carl.

A few moments later he answers. He's still wearing yesterday's t-shirt and the same stained pants. Maybe the same funked boxers. He didn't even bother with more deodorant.

"Not you both," he says.

Noble doesn't give Carl a chance to shut the door without pushing his way past the guy.

"I don't want you to quit the fraternity," I tell him.

He climbs onto his bed, until his back is to the wall. "If I stay, it would be awkward between us. It could happen again. We shouldn't have ... I shouldn't have let it happen."

"I'm sorry. I took advantage of you."

Noble turns the only chair in the room around and sits down to watch us. If he had popcorn, he'd be snacking right now.

"No," Carl says. He glances at Noble a moment. "I know the way some of them treat you. I felt ... I wanted to show that not everyone there wants to hurt you."

"You're the only reason I've been able to stay. If you leave, there's nothing left for me."

"Aww, such a tender moment," Noble says. "Brought to you by the good folks at Zeta Psi."

I want to approach Carl, sit beside him, offer comfort, but I'm the one that caused him real pain. "We can forget the attic. Pretend it never happened. Noble won't say anything about it, right?"

Noble leans back, making the chair squeak in protest. "Of course. Carl, you don't want to abandon your friend? All your friends? Pledging can be hard. One down, and so few left to pick up the slack. Without you, it'll be really hard on Sippy."

"Steve. His name is Steve."

"Well, you don't want me to pass Steve around to the other brothers like he's a Tri-Delt sister? Do you?"

"Can you be, for once, less of asshole?" I say.

Carl's neck is taut as he stares at Noble.

I step into his line of sight and gesture at my heart, as if reciting a pledge of allegiance. "The only thing I want is us to be friends again. Don't say 'Yes,' because of him, say 'Yes,' because of me. Not to save me, not to protect me, just because I need you there to talk to me every day, to walk home with me every night."

"Okay," Carl says. The word slips out, low but fast, as if it were on the tip of his tongue.

Noble smacks his hands together. "Terrific." He stands up, letting the chair topple. "This calls for a toast." He reaches into his pocket and brings out the Bailey flask.

"Fuck you," I tell him.

He *tsk-tsks* me "One little sip can't do harm. Unless what you put in here—"

And the idea ignites in my brain, burns fast from weeks of kindling—insults and snide remarks, threats, slaps and cuts, and his groping in the shower. "You first."

His smirk falters, but he unscrews the cap.

I catch a whiff of Malört. "It's your favorite, after all."

Carl groans. "I don't know how you can stomach that. It tastes like you wiped a toilet with a lime, then soaked it in moonshine."

And I actually reach out to Carl, to hold on to his shoulder, to gesture my thanks for saying something that would gall Noble to lift the Bailey flask to his lips and drink.

I admit I'm curious to see what will happen.

Noble soon tilts his head back, shifts the flask so it's vertical, and his swollen Adam's apple bounces under the skin as he keeps swallowing and swallowing.

Carl grabs my arm. We're watching amber liquor pour down his face. I don't know if he's even breathing anymore.

My fingers pry at the hand holding the Bailey flask. He doesn't seem to notice we're there. The smell is awful; Carl calls out that Noble's pissing himself, maybe to make more room; he's saturated, we're becoming soaked, and I glimpse his eyes are wide but rolled back, like a shark's, only the dull white showing.

When we succeed in taking the flask from him, he falls limp in a puddle that's formed on the carpet.

Carl's holding up Noble's head, checking to make sure the airway is clear. Noble takes a long, deep, haggard breath.

"I think I should get the resident advisor," I say.

"He looks bad."

Noble shakes and stumbles, but makes it to his feet. He's looking at the window, which night has turned into one long, dark mirror.

I catch him whispering, "What did you say?"

"You look bad."

He grins. Only it's so stretched that there's no humor on his face. "No. I'm ... I'm handsome as all-fuck."

He pushes us away and rushes at his reflection. I cringe at the sound of his face striking the glass. Fireworks of blood stipple the window, silhouette his head as he begins what I first think is trying to eat the pane, but soon realize by the way he's licking and nipping the window, is him trying to kiss his reflection.

"Shit, oh, shit," Carl says.

Noble smacks the glass with one hand. Then his face cracks the pane. Bones cracks too. Part of a tooth is glued by gore to the glass. He's trying to undress, to free himself of damp jeans, like an eager drunk.

"Go get the RA," I tell Carl. "I'll call campus security." But I find I don't have my phone on me, being the good pledge for once, so I have to run out into the hall as it fills with students attracted to the nose.

I imagine cracks in the glass becoming an active cobweb with Noble trapped in the center. But only for moment.

CARL'S NURSING A SODA AS he sits on the stiff couch on the third-floor lounge. People in uniforms have come and gone, and it's near midnight when we're finally alone together.

Carl hasn't spoken about what happened. Not unless answering a question. Now his silence is awful.

I touch the top of his head. "You can't go back there." It's true; the room is locked and covered in yellow tape.

He shakes his head. "No, I can't."

I sit beside him. "Come back to my dorm room."

He looks up at me. His fingers twist at the pull tab until it pries loose.

"You can have my bed, and I'll sleep on the floor."

He agrees and I lead him to the elevator. He moves like a sleepwalker.

Jairo knows—everyone in the building, maybe campus, knows by now—and he rushes over and gives us both hugs. Carl accepts this, from a stranger, as if family, burying his head into the crook of Jairo's neck.

"I said he could sleep here. Take my bed."

"Of course." Jairo rubs Carl's arm. "But first, I think a hot shower?"

"I have some clothes—"

Jairo mouths *Slow down* to me. "He can borrow mine." Jairo begins rummaging through the closet.

Carl drifts over to my elephant. He lifts it up, shakes it once. "Is it candy?"

I'm about to say "No," when Jairo steps on my shoe. "Of course." He looks at me. "Why don't you change those sheets so the bed is as clean as Carl will be when I bring him back?"

"Got it."

I AM SURPRISED, WITH CARL being inches away, that I can even fall asleep, but I'm awoken by the gentle touch of his fingers brushing my bare arm.

"Hmm?" I turn onto my back. He's looking down at me, face slightly mushed by the mattress.

"It was drugs, right?" he whispers.

I nod. *How can I ever explain everything without losing him?*

"I wanted to."

"Wanted to what?"

He sighs. I take hold of one of his fingers and repeat the question.

"Kiss you in the attic. I thought about it as I was climbing up after you."

"Oh."

"I was afraid you wouldn't want me to. You're the best friend I have. Back home all the guys that I thought were friends, they were like the guys at the fraternity, all talk, but did they really care about me?" He curls our fingers together. "I want someone to worry whether I'm still breathing every day. Maybe that's more than a friend. Maybe because I see you every day."

"Are you okay?"

He thinks a while. I revel in the feel of his hand, so warm.

"If I invited you up here." He bites his lip. "In your bed—"

"Together."

"Would you say 'Yes'?"

I untangle myself from the sheet covering me. The bed is so small, and with all our limbs I should feel as confined as the attic. But the air-conditioning is on high, sending a breeze over both of us, and I can press my face into the soft locks of his hair and smell whatever organic shampoo Jairo must buy. And then Carl moves, and we're staring into each other's faces, waiting to see whose lips will come closer first. My breath lingers in my chest, and I'm worried there will be tears. Maybe from him. Maybe from me.

But his lips aren't salty, and his mouth tastes sweeter than any I have known.

BOTTOM OF THE MENU

S TANDING OUTSIDE THE RESTAURANT, I pause to watch for a minute
or so the young man leaning against a parking meter as he smokes
a cigarette. As his face is turned away from me toward the lowering
sun, all I can see is a carefully maintained mane of loose brown curls. He has
a mesomorphic build complemented by a long-sleeved, ribbed t-shirt and
worn denim jeans. His not texting or talking on a cell phone is an anomaly;
when was the last time you saw someone under the age of thirty, all alone
and idle, without the ubiquitous handhelds clutched with devotion? Likely,
the young man's battery died and now he finds himself confronted with the
realizations a moment of solitude brings. Pity no one daydreams any more.

I know I am a sarcastic queen. But on my forty-fourth birthday, I have
license.

I walk to the front glass windows of Stylus, and peer inside at the many
small tables, nearly all filled at that hour. A puff of bitter smoke reaches me
along with the words, "You must be Mr. Berman."

The young man's face, is clean-shaven and naturally tan with a small
nose almost lost above his wide mouth, which grins in the moment. Nicotine
has tinted his teeth a bit, but whenever an aging queen admires youth, he
must be forgiving of imperfections.

"I might be."

He transfers the lit cigarette to his left hand before holding out the right. "I'm Baker. The menu."

"The baker?"

He chuckles. "No, no. Baker's my name. But I am the menu."

I presume he's flirting, an unprecedented hustler on this street that doesn't have much gay traffic, unlike 12th or 13th. I thank him for whatever overture and step to the brass-and-wood door of Stylus. He moves faster and holds it open for me, then follows after.

Meager air-conditioning that fails to dispel most of the summer heat greets us both. Old-fashioned, belt-driven fans cautiously spin just shy of the ceiling. But the hostess is untitled and bounces our way. "Welcome to Stylus, Mr. Berman."

A TRICKLE OF DREAD CURDLES my empty stomach as I worry if my nephew has orchestrated tonight something more elaborate that a free dinner. The last thing I want is the attention of strangers, an entire restaurant full of turned, curious faces, all cruelly aware of the fact I am dining *alone* on my *birthday*. I should have postponed any and all celebrations until my friends returned to town from their summer vacations. Not even my favorite nephew could attend; rumor from the family switchboard suggests he's found yet another horrendous job that he thinks will change the world.

"I see you have met your menu." She motions like a beauty queen towards the youth beside me, who must have abandoned his cigarette outside.

"He's never had the special before," Baker says and then leans in to kiss the hostess on the cheek.

She echoes Baker's grin, though it looks less than charming the second time. "You *are* in for an unexpected treat then, Mr. Berman."

"My table?"

She leads us—Baker has seen fit to place a hand lightly on my lower back—to a table toward the rear of the restaurant but not too close to the kitchen. Baker pulls out my seat for me. I suppose even hustlers must now go to school for etiquette. I shall have to revise my view of the twenty-first century's mores.

The hostess does not offer menus to either of us, though. She rushes to greet another patron before I can mention this oversight. I glance around and other expectant diners are ordering off folded paper menus.

"I know what you are thinking," Baker says.

I raise an eyebrow and lean forward. The round table is a mite small, swallowed up by glasses, bread plates, cutlery and napkins, let alone my elbows. "All of what I am thinking? You're a magician, then."

"Of sorts." He rolls up the sleeve of his left arm. "What would you like to drink?" His entire forearm is covered in black ink. Tattooed script, fine calligraphy. I peer closer and read *Vieux Carré = Rye whiskey & Cognac & Sweet Vermouth & Benedictine w/ dashes of Angostura & Peychauds / Broken Halo = Plymouth Gin & Dry Sack & Williams Humbert & Oloroso w/ Maraschino liqueur / Witch Doctor = Malibu coconut rum & Reposado tequila w/ pineapple juice & orange juice & Meyer lemon juice.*

"I ... I'm at a loss for words." Unlike apparently the menu. I dare to reach out to touch his inked forearm. The young skin is smooth and warm, like the burn of good Cognac. And my fingers linger a moment over *Vieux Carré.*

"Deux Vieux Carré," Baker calls out to a waitress passing by.

I cannot begrudge him a drink. The gift certificate, printed on creamy, thick stock, arrived in the old-fashioned mail yesterday, offered only the restaurant's street address and the time of my reservation. AJ's handwriting was clear on the outer envelope.

"Now your appetizer." He exposes his right forearm. "I recommend the green mussels gratinés." His fingertip underlines the rest of the dish: *Dijon butter, sweet sausage crumbs.*

"How often do you do this?"

He opens his mouth to speak but the waitress interrupts him as she sets down our drinks.

I raise my glass of liquid French Quarter. My alma mater, Tulane, would be proud of me. "Don't tell me. If you answered 'All the time,' I'd be more perplexed than disappointed—how come I have never heard of walking, handsome menus."

"And if I said 'never'?" he asks before a sip.

"Then I would feel most awkward that someone tattooed their body for me. I'm not that special."

"But today makes you special—"

I clink my glass against his own. "As well as the other umpteen number of men and women born today. Shania Twain. A Japanese composer. The author Jack Vance. Oh, and Jason Priestly. There once was a time when a guy might get inked to impress Jason Priestly. I think the only thing you had on your skin in the nineties was baby powder."

Baker laughs. "You're not a fossil. If I told you I had 'dry-aged beef' tattooed across my chest, you would make some remark about—"

"About myself." I shrug. "Guilty." I realize I have steadily sipped my drink down to the bottom and can feel the early euphoria of alcohol loosening my thoughts. "I can't say I'm used to outré presents."

"You can say whatever you want. Until the entrée. After your first taste, you're allowed no questions."

The waitress returns. Or the hostess. Or maybe the hostess's twin. They all look so similar. I order the mussels and two more drinks.

"So, the entrée …" Baker begins removing his t-shirt. I feel flushed, from the alcohol, from the sight of someone attractive committing a cardinal sin: No Shoes, No Shirts, No Service! I lean back in my chair, as if to distance myself from him, and nearly topple.

None of the other Stylus patrons stop and stare; they continue handling their forks and knives and spoons, all the while chattering and gossiping. I wonder if Baker (now shirtless—and how his illuminated chest glistens with a bit of August sweat) and I have been seated in some odd section of the restaurant burdened with something akin to bad acoustics but affecting all the senses. I drop my knife. It clatters against the wood floor. A woman seated nearby glares. She could be the hostess's sister, they look so much alike, down to the same highlights in her hair.

"Steve, do you like chicken?"

I mean to search Baker's face for guile but the path his fingers make as they caress the damp skin of his chest draws my gaze: the black lettering askew as it flows over a pec, down the vale, then rises again, a carnival trick for the ages.

"Here you can indulge …" He takes my hand and guides it to the ink, as if it were Braille.

Pygostyle in spicy ginger sauce w/ sautéed kale & carrots
Green pasillas stuffed with criadillas w/ black beans & rice
Welsh faggot & marrowfat peas

I want to lick the drops of sweat my fingers catch underneath the word *marrowfat.* Would they taste salty? Sour? Have I drank too much Cognac and rye to even discern a new taste?

"Your mussels," says the waitress and sets a plate between us.

"The portions here," Baker says (do his eyes drift to the plate or down to his crotch?), "are generous. So we'll share."

I bite a mussel—delicious—but not the muscle I want. Oh, I am tipsy. I may have even said this aloud because Baker is chuckling as if I said something whimsical but suggestive. My appetite extends beyond the seafood. I want to nibble on his unkempt hair, test the thickness of the cords at his neck, lick and see if the ink is nothing more than food coloring artfully applied.

Oh, what a generous nephew I have!

But my gratitude is suddenly tempered by doubt. Twenty-two and resentful, AJ never pays for a meal if he has to; a proud freegan, he regularly raids dumpsters and brings back the salvage to the dilapidated building where he squats with three other roommates of doubtful hygiene. How could he even afford to buy me such a meal?

"You're not a friend of AJ's, are you?" If so, Baker would be one of the Untouchable caste.

"No. We've never met."

I have not spoken to AJ since the funeral. He hasn't returned my calls or emails. I had no idea he even knew my birthday.

When the pygostyle arrives, Baker cuts the meat and offers me the first bite, the fork held to my lips. It's the gesture of young love, of hearts worn on sleeves, a gesture that repulses cynics like a crucifix brandished before a vampire. He notes my hesitation. He cocks his head. "Relax, no one is watching."

"I find that hard to believe."

"Honest. Watch." He sets the fork down, balancing it at the edge of the hot dish. He pushes his chair back and stands up. "No menu is complete without listing desserts and digestifs." He unbuttons the top of his jeans and pushes his palms past the waistband, revealing a trail of unruly hair.

Why is no one staring? *I am staring.* Why no one else?

"It's your birthday," he says, sitting back down. "Don't question, don't worry. Have a good meal."

"Asking if you are a daydream would be questioning."

"Yep." He holds up the fork.

I want the chicken to be like pomegranate seeds in Hades, keeping me with Baker for months out of every year. But the taste, potent, savory, does not linger past another sip of Cognac that I don't remember ordering anew.

"I'm drunk."

"Good," he says. "You'll be less skeptical."

"I want to know what happens when I get to the end of the meal."

"You do?" He offers me another forkful. I am so eager to take a bite that my teeth hit metal.

"So," Baker asks, "have you ever gotten laid on your birthday?"

The bold question chokes me. "N-No. Not my birthday." Why is there nothing but alcohol to clear my throat? "On Halloween, many, many years ago, I blew a boy in my car. In a graveyard. Full moon, too. And one New Year's Eve in New Orleans I went down on a guy in the middle of a crowded dance floor." The memories rush back, filling spaces in my head like the potent vapors rising from the glass at my lips.

He fluffs his curls a moment. "You like to spend your holidays with your mouth full."

I spill a bit of my drink when I start braying. It seems harder to consider my words, to not ask a question, for it not to be something so raunchy that I fear it would clatter like the dropped knife.

He takes a finger and dips it into the sauce. Slow. Even slower, he lifts it to his lips and sucks the tip clean. I have begun to salivate anew.

"The cook here told me that melting a piece of chocolate in your mouth affects your brain. Lights up the grey matter like you were kissing someone."

"Then I better hope chocolate is on the dessert menu."

"Eager for dessert?"

I nod. Not that the food at Stylus isn't delicious ....

He leans back in his chair and gestures for me to stand and come close. "You have to open it."

I sway when I stand. A passing waitress—perhaps its the same one I see, perhaps Stylus employs a troupe of identical triplets—winks at me. My napkin lands on the floor. I must not step on it. I must not trip as I walk around the table and kneel in front of Baker.

I take my time unbuttoning his jeans. I have to. I think my hands are

176

trembling. I see the coarse hair of his slightly rounded stomach reach the band of a bleached-white jockstrap. He lifts his ass to let me slide the butter-soft denim down to pool at his feet, and I can see running up his left thigh mention of the desserts:

Red banana confit w/ Moscata d'Asti

"In Central America they think the sap of the red banana tree is an aphrodisiac." Baker adjusts the swollen front of his jockstrap.

Fresh pound cake w/ confiture de lait

My mouth has grown dry as my mother's pound cake. And how much the faygele am I to be thinking about my mother while on my knees before a crotch?

Chocolate Scoville, assorted cacao squares dusted w/ variety of dried pepper flakes

"A bite of that chocolate would be a very torrid kiss," I say.

"Singe your lips. Blister your tongue."

On his right thigh are the digestifs, which I just glance at. I don't need any more alcohol. But I do run a hand over that leg. I squeeze the flesh, the bony cap of knee. He smells a bit sweaty.

"I can't decide. Order for me." But not deciding is most definitely a choice.

He reaches down and strokes my hair. "That would be against the rules."

I almost ask, "There are rules? Still? To all this wonder?" but he prevents me by moving his fingers down my face to press shut my lips.

"There are always rules. And a price. Your nephew paid that so you could play with me here. Those are the rules."

His mention of AJ chastens my besotted thoughts. At the funeral he seemed more aggrieved than grieving. He sullenly refused to present at the cremation. And I became irritated with this showing. Words were spoken outside the funeral parlor as his mother burned bright.

I feel a sinking sense that I failed him by even mentioning the letters D-N-R.

"I once wrote a story about an oven that came to life and ate German children. Never finished one about a were-oven. I don't know why I am obsessed with ovens. I don't even cook at home ... maybe I've used the oven three times in all the years I've lived in the apartment."

"It's not unusual to be fear being burned. But the management prides itself on moral certainty."

I suspect that is the first lie he has told me. "They say presentation matters." I sigh and rub again his legs. "I'll have the confit. Too much pepper and I'll worry about burning my throat."

I return to my seat. I do not step on my napkin. I don't want anyone to pay a heavy price for my sake. I wonder if I could walk out. If the meal is already paid for ... but no, I'm already too entranced.

"The confit is still very tasty," Baker says. He reaches out but I busy my hands in my pants pockets—no, not to adjust myself but to get my wallet. I pull out the gift certificate. Maybe the waitress heard my choice because a moment later she is there with the plate. It looks tempting. She plucks the certificate from my hand.

I could laugh at all this. Baker, though incredibly attractive, a feast for the eyes, does look a bit ridiculous with his pants down. I've drunk enough to laugh. I wonder if there is still one last bit of the menu that hasn't been revealed, inked and hidden underneath a layer of taut cotton.

He nods at me. "Finish the meal." His tone is almost stern.

I scoop up a bit of the confit, which is blood-red and drips off the spoon to splatter my slacks. Baker watches me. His stare thickens the air so it seems forever before I taste the dessert. Its sweetness is cloying and warm, reminding me of the cheap raspberry tarts my other sister brought to the *shiva*. I suspected she found them at a convenience store on the drive over.

Baker smirks as he stands and pulls up his jeans. "There's a spot, just behind the kitchen. The ovens, actually. The brick walls hold the heat well, much like a sauna, so you have to strip bare before going inside." He throws his t-shirt on the floor, where it lands next to my napkin. "A tour comes with the meal." He holds out a hand to me.

As I follow his lead, I glance once more around me. Out the window, another young man dressed in scroungy chic has taken over the exact spot where I first saw Baker. While his head is turned toward the horizon, his stance is familiar. I hesitate a moment, an apology on my lips, but then Baker tugs my arm, and without much resistance I follow into the kitchen, the oven, whatever might happen there.

AFTERWORD

THANK YOU TO MY READERS. Thank you to the editors who bought these stories.

A number of kind friends critiqued the stories in this book. A smaller number of them are still speaking to me.

I consider my mother an excellent cook and my father an inspiration because he was never afraid of any dish (he tried Rocky Mountain Oysters before his son ever dared a testicle). Though neither of them will ever read this page or the ones before it, I am eternally indebted to both of them.

I'm grateful to the fine folk at an elegant, little Italian restaurant in Bayonne: Years ago, when I was a professional book buyer, publishers' sales reps introduced me to Cafe Bello, which soon became my favorite place to dine, but soon I was being taken there three or four times a week for two-hour lunches, so my boss told me the place was verboten, which didn't stop me from going there for early suppers, one of many reasons why this will always be my favorite day job, one I regretted leaving, but it was Bayonne, after all, and I was young and foolish. On my last night, my coworkers treated me to Cafe Bello one last time, and the staff presented me with a bottle of fine wine in gratitude and recognition for all the business I brought them.

My inspiration began with the efforts of Cora Emmeline Greaves: She struggled for years to finish and promote her cookbook *The Emprise, The Entrée*, with little success until she convinced a Paternoster Row bookseller to let her sit in the storefront at a small desk and eat her typewriter a little bit at a time, often without benefit of condiments, and Cora soon drew crowds, who peered at her through the glass during much of October in 1903, with an encore performance at King's College Hospital. How could I not persevere with my own writing?

Writing these stories, I was sustained by some of my favorited foods: bastard potatoes, squat lobsters, huckleberries on beef, black, and white milkshakes.

And thank you for rice pudding, the perfect creamy off-white medium for hiding semen. The dessert was one of my college roommate's favorites, and I conceived revenge after the last beating. I remember him looking so cruelly handsome lounging on the sofa in only his flannel boxers and feeding himself greedy spoonfuls of the stuff. *Odi at amo,* I whispered as he cleaned the bowl with his thumb, sucking it clean.

I should also thank that young man from South Korea for not murdering me. We met at bar in New Orleans, a night prior to New Year's Eve. His English was limited, but we soon realized that we were hungry for each other, yet neither of us could bring the other back to our room (he stayed at a youth hostel, while I shared a hotel room with family). Libido being a sibling to necessity and the reason for much invention, I thought myself clever enough to ask a cab driver where he would take the local prostitutes with their clients. Off we sped to a bleak, almost-Brutalist motel in a part of the city I had never seen before. So I asked the cab driver to idle, and in we went. I paid for the room, which was a generous term for the space, with its bare mattress and chipped porcelain sink and nothing else. We stripped down, and then he straddled me. But his kisses stopped after a minute or two, and the hands that had been stroking my hair, my chest, went to my neck. One hand went to my throat, the other pushed up my chin. He looked at me as if I was something disagreeable, something far worse than a complete stranger. *Are you Jewish?* he asked me and his grip tightened. I remained calm, and I lied. And then we fucked, because I felt certain that the rage simmering inside him would not take kindly if I rolled him off me and said I wasn't feeling the moment any more. After finishing each other off, he became languid, the strength lost to all his limbs. He stared at me as I hastily dressed. I mumbled something about taking the cab back to the French Quarter. Reunited with my siblings at the hotel, they asked me where I'd been. My answer was the second, but far less momentous, deception of the night. The menace, the trauma, were only expunged when I told the story to dear friends.

And thanks, too, to the mortuary student I took to dinner. He appealed to my macabre interests and resembled one of the rugby players in a Benetton ad. I wanted him to tell me between kisses how does one make a corpse look pretty. I wanted him to leave my lips raw. He slurped and swallowed his way through the menu, his mouth open wide as he chewed and explaining livor mortis. Every so often he would slip greasy fingers into the corners of his mouth and retrieve a bit of gristle or bone, which he placed on the white tablecloth beside his plate, a practice I first witnessed in China. The span of fabric between us soon became dappled a ruddy pink. He excused himself to the bathroom when the waiter brought the check. I dawdled at the table as the plates were cleared, knocking one of the detritus almost into my lap. I was about to brush it aside when I realized it was a tooth, a back tooth. I spilled water on the others, clearing sauce and blood. All of them teeth.

PUBL;ICATION CREDITS